Tides of Desire A Soldier's Canvas

Tides of Love: Military

Lilly Grace Nash

Published by JL Lam Publishing, 2024.

This is a work of fiction. Similarities to real people, places, or events are entirely coincidental.

TIDES OF DESIRE A SOLDIER'S CANVAS

First edition. October 20, 2024.

Copyright © 2024 Lilly Grace Nash.

ISBN: 979-8227830128

Written by Lilly Grace Nash.

Also by Lilly Grace Nash

Courting Justice
Alliances & Betrayals
The Billionaire's Legal Affair
Objection to Love
Love's Final Exoneration

SEALs of Love Romance
Undercover Hearts
Fractured Hearts
Healing Hearts

Second Chance Romance
Damaged Ex-SEAL's Second Chance
Ex-SEAL's Second Chance

Tides of Love: Military

Tides of Desire A Soldier's Canvas

Standalone
Billionaire's Nanny Fake Marriage
Silent Hearts, Secret Desires
Boss Daddy's Nanny

Watch for more at https://jllampublishing.com/lilly-grace-nash.

Table of Contents

Return to the Quiet Shores	1
Brushstrokes and Beginnings	9
Echoes and Awakenings	17
Whispers of the Heart	24
Under the Summer Stars	29
Blooms of the Heart	36
Shadows and Light	43
Building Foundations	51
The Farewell	57
Unforeseen Colors	63
Echoes Through the Jungle: A Promise Unyielded	77
Colors of Resilience: Embracing the Unknown	86
Echoes of the Forgotten	98
Awaiting Dawn	109
Awakening Memories	118
Reclaimed Horizons	130
New Beginnings, Shared Dreams	146
Brushstrokes of Forever	163
Canvas of Love and Healing	172
A Soldier's Canvas	181

To my beloved husband,

whose unwavering support, endless encouragement, and steadfast belief in me have been the guiding light throughout my journey.

Your love is the foundation upon which I build my dreams.

Return to the Quiet Shores

Shane

Home. As I stepped off the train into the sparse cinderblock depot, I drew in a deep breath of humid Georgia air that somehow smelled like home – pine, grass, and nostalgia. The two stern-faced privates trailing my heels may as well have been tourist attractions themselves, awkwardly ogling this quaint town that rarely hosted soldiers graced with guns and combat boots.

"At ease, gentlemen. My aunt's Cavalier will do for the half-hour trek to basecamp," I dismissed them, anxious for some hard-earned alone time this leave. Nothing personal of course – after six relentless years serving in MARSOC alongside more valor and sacrifice than civilians could conceive, twelve weeks stateside was a godsend. Still, a week bunking on hangar cots at Pendleton with those wet-nosed kids was enough before I went stir crazy. Three days into my cross-country freedom and I already itched for seclusion that only the old family cottage could provide.

I watched the camouflaged duo scan the platform uncertainly. Bless 'em, they were as displaced here as tuxedos at a hog roast. The cabbie shot me a knowing smirk and drawled, "'Bout time y'all let this young man come home an' give him some peace. I'll be sure someone picks ya up when your leave's up." Private Michaels flushed, grabbing their duffels.

"Yes sir, Sergeant Cooper! We'll report to Base 1700 hours at summer's end." Still grinning, I offered the cabbie a crisp twenty with a nod of thanks. No need to embarrass Michaels further for following orders. Besides, I appreciated the diligence given recent events.

As the olive taxi chugged off towards Warner Robins, the familiar silence restored calm. Silence – now an old friend after years of 60-round bursts shattering the night, blazing helicopters fanning the stench of sweat and blood until we choked, cries cutting through the darkness...No, I cut off memories now rising unbidden. I was home, free of that for twelve glorious weeks.

Glancing around the weathered platform, I realized not much had changed, still an echo of simpler times. The faded Coca Cola mural slogan "Delicious and Refreshing!" now sadly ironic given they closed the bottling plant after the war. Old Clarence's newsstand stood wooden and stalwart; I'd start my break reading Zane Grey novels just as I did back when. And perched among scattered benches sat the original analog clock, still faithfully ticking despite wristwatches and smartphones overtaking today's pace. The familiarity swaddled me like the old quilts Gramma draped on our laps during evening stories – comforting, worn, and mine.

I hitched my duffel higher and headed towards the dirt parking lot, nary a civilian glancing up from their smartphones. My polished low-quarters skimmed the patched macadam out front, remnants of youth spent burning rubber out of this place most weekends. Whether bombing back roads with a sixer of cold ones stuffed with buddies or peeling into Makeout Point with Jessie Knox hot on my heels, some wilder memories indelibly marked this soil. Well before convoys and secret missions carved deeper, bloodier tracks across my years.

As the familiar silence of Wesleyan Woods wrapped around me, echoes of the past whispered through the crisp air, reminding me of the boy who once dreamt beneath these vast, Georgia skies. I was never meant to be a small-town hero, content with the predictable path of taking over the family hardware store. Instead, I was drawn to the allure of making a difference on a global stage, fueled by the tales of valor and sacrifice my grandfather shared from his own service in Korea. Those stories, imbued with a sense of purpose and camaraderie, lit a fire in me that Jefferson Hills could never contain.

Joining MARSOC wasn't just about escaping the confines of a predestined life; it was a pledge to myself and to the memory of my parents. I sought to be part of something larger, to protect the ideals they had fought for, and to forge my path through sheer will and determination. But the reality of service, of war, was a crucible that reshaped me in ways I hadn't anticipated. Each mission, each life-or-death decision, stripped away layers of who I thought I was, revealing a core tempered by adversity and companionship.

I learned the true meaning of sacrifice, not as an abstract concept glorified in war stories, but as a painful, personal ordeal witnessed in the eyes of brothers-in-arms who laid down their lives with a quiet dignity that left me humbled and forever changed. The camaraderie formed in the crucible of conflict became my anchor, teaching me the value of trust, loyalty, and the unspoken bond that forms when you rely on someone else for your very survival.

These experiences, the blend of loss and brotherhood, etched deep into my soul, fueling a relentless drive to make each moment count, for those who could no longer seize theirs.

Yet, they also left a yearning for peace, a peace I now sought in the familiar, yet distant, embrace of home.

As I stood on the threshold of the family cottage, a flood of memories greeted me, but so did the shadows of men I could not save, their whispered laughter like ghosts in the wind. Here, in the quiet of Wesleyan Woods, I hoped to find solace, to reconcile the man I had become with the boy who once dreamt of glory beneath these stars.

Cresting the last hill where Granddad's prized silver Kingswood wagon rusted in weeds, the tired cottage sagged against a pastel sky. I halted, hit with an odd pang seeing the place so lonesome. When I left for duty six years back they were both still kicking – Granddad stoking the wood-burning stove he built, Gramma's lavender tea cakes welcoming me home after late nights. Watching them gently bicker about politics over the evening crossword, her slipper lightly nudging his only to elicit some cheek. Thirty years wed and still sweet on one another. Even when she got sick, he cared for her proudly until the chemo stole her blue eyes, rubbing her feet as they faded. Then six months later to the day, Granddad was discovered slumped at her grave, the Kingswood keys clutched cold in his hand.

My throat suddenly thickened. Those two were supposed to live forever, their love carved into these unshakable Macon foothills. I still expected to smell Gramma's rosewater greeting me instead of musty disuse. Grief ambushed me at odd moments, even though they had passed years ago. Despite death engraving itself daily into our reality overseas, losing my closest kin gut-punched me. Like the terrain you rappelled flawlessly for years unexpectedly crumbling, leaving you winded and flailing.

I slowly walked up mottled stone steps they'd descended a thousand times, each creak familiar. The faded periwinkle door still dangled a rusted horseshoe – remnants of Gramma's fanciful wishing for luck. If only their four-leafed clovers and white feathers guarded us all a bit longer. My fingers traced the ruts where sometime last fall a bear tried busting this old door open. Probably desperate for one last nibble of Gramma's blackberry preserves before hibernation. Can't say I blame him; no one could make a treat spark magic amid the mundane like her. I wonder if whoever empties the place will discover dusty jars still lining root cellar shelves, unopened presents from her ever-giving heart.

Unlocking three stubborn deadbolts, I pushed inside the musty stillness once housing my only sense of home. Stripes of sunlight fell across oak planks scuffed by years of workingman's boots and pattering young feet. Bits of leaves and field dust skittered across the creaking floor, no slippered matron tidying anymore. The hand-whittled coat rack stood akimbo by the door, no jackets keeping it company besides the wool hunting coat I outgrew sophomore year. Tongues of lace curtains hung listlessly dormant without Gramma tsking about blasts of winter air let inside. Quiet as a church, if churches build altars with well-loved La-Z-boy recliners.

I dropped my pack feeling vaguely sacrilegious disturbing hallowed remnants now tomb-like. It sank in that I alone remained tied to this place, imprinted with pieces of me from first fishing lessons to awkward first dates. Assessing the musty living room, I suddenly questioned if I should stay or if being surrounded by ghosts worsened the grief. I could get a motel, avoid stirring sentimentality and get properly drunk off duty.

Just then the antique schoolhouse clock chimed five from the hall as it had my entire life. I exhaled, the familiar refrain anchoring me. However it looked now with their loss, these walls were built by people who loved unyieldingly. Who stoked my spirit for brighter horizons beyond this town, but sheltered my soul when I fell short. I couldn't envision better companionship to grapple with the chaos witnessed overseas if this leave granted me the chance to reclaim my humanity and make sense of everything seen in the fury of war. I walked over and opened the drapes, streaking evening gold into the hushed space. The motes shimmered to life, dancing across Granddad's battered TV trays that somehow survived each spring purge. That small movement returned breath, purpose. They may have vacated the worn structure, but it was my turn now to occupy the cottage, imbuing suppers and stories that warmed generations uncounted. That was honoring love's legacy – inhabiting not entombing, sharing that light where darkness threatens.

My melancholy lifted, buoyed by purpose. I raided musty cupboards finding vintage hurricane lamps left ready to be lit once more. The cherry Frigidaire wheezed worryingly but surrendered a lone Schlitz tallboy and foil-wrapped cookies that made me smile discovering Gramma's spidery signature – Welcome Home Shane! My girl thinks ahead. I assembled mismatched dishes from the 1950s, the same I smeared with mess as a boy yet now handled reverently. As the evening softened into dusk, I fired up Granddad's temperamental but trusty grill, the sizzling burgers welcoming me home as much as the crickets serenading the first tasty bite. Three months here suddenly seemed a gift instead of an inadequate break from combat abroad. Years of training conditioned me to catch sleep wherever possible – bedrolls on frozen mountain sides, desert camo tents, bombed out tenements – so settling into the lumpy sleeper couch felt like checking into a luxury suite. Donning faded jeans and my unit's T-shirt, icy beer in hand, I headed the quarter mile downhill through field grass to Pop's favorite fishing hole. Night sounds buzzed hypnotically as I settled in watching fireflies winking along the silty shore.

I tipped my face back as the night sky swelled endless above me, stars vibrant and pulsing stronger than any I'd witnessed around the globe. As a Marine you experience celestial majesty everywhere – the Southern Cross's blaze over the Tasman Sea, the emerald dance of northern lights over Korean winters, Saharan sands shifting under the Milky Way's pour. I'd marveled at the heavens' glory shining even through suffering on battlefields.

Yet sprawled on this unremarkable grass by a lackluster fishing hole, the constellations emerged profound and new. What made this evening firmament so extraordinary as it arched over home soil? Perhaps witnessing inhumanity abroad expanded mystery's power, humbling even battle-hardened leathernecks like myself. Or maybe ten years serving afforded new eyes, awakening child-like wonder muted through decades' loss.

I searched the glittering tableau, identifying Orion, the Dippers, Cassiopeia...memories flickering like projector slides across my mind's eye. Hazy summer nights studying astronomy to impress Rose Gulden before she kissed Stephen Mills behind the Dairy Freeze. Furious meteors streaking overhead as we crouched terrified in Iraqi trenches when the bombs fell too close. Helpless as we watched dawn's rosy fingers claw from the night sky after Taliban ambushes, holding brothers who wouldn't see another sunrise.

My chest hitched recognizing every point of light symbolized unrealized dreams and liberated souls swirling unseen. As a familiar peace settled within, my ribs gradually unclenched from constant vigilance. Ten years worth of violence and grit slowly sloughed off my soul. Maybe that's what coming home truly meant...not locating a particular house you once loved, but rediscovering stillness within all the chaos. My shoulders eased and I breathed freer than I had in ages, blessed by small miracles most overlook.

Above the summer chorus, the schoolhouse clock chimed ten. Twelve weeks' leave abruptly seemed inadequate time to reclaim life with ghosts I loved under these brilliant stars. I should gather the gardening tools tomorrow, coaxing Gramma's roses back to bloom before I shipped out again.

Brushstrokes and Beginnings

Emily

Lights of filtered pink and orange hues through my sheer curtains, rousing me gently from dreams saturated with vibrant azure waves crashing along sandy Atlantic shores. As a child, my sisters Lily, Elaine and I vacationed on Rhode Island beach with our art-loving mother and steadfast Georgian father in his stalwart Carhartts. Their devotion not just towards each other but nurturing creativity in their inquisitive daughters established my foundation as firmly as the old oaks rimming our rambling farmhouse.

Even now as adults with Lily having her own rambunctious boys to chase onshore, we sisters wandered tidal pools examining sculptural qualities of weathered driftwood and glittering sea glass. Nowadays I rose habitually with the birds, as eager as my nephews for possibility. As an artist, I studied the dancing shadow patterns on my rumpled sheets, visualizing a future painting. I wanted to recreate not just the mesmerizing sunlight, but the deeper meaning it evoked within me. These quiet moments brought back the youthful creative joy I nearly lost during my dramatic, painful teen years. Observing nature's small miracles revived my childlike wonder that fuels meaningful art. My fingers twitched with anticipation, eager to grasp my brushes again to capture elusive beauty. Stilling my mind allowed inspiration to flow untainted by grown-up worries that restrict imagination. I slipped on an oversized Eagles jersey inherited from Lily's linebacker high school boyfriend and padded barefoot downstairs. A neat row of finished birch wood carvings lined the entryway – whimsical dogs, patient bears, ballerinas frozen mid-pirouette. My neighbor Mr. O'Reilly, retired Bibb County detective now woodworking artisan, gifted me with treasures whenever inspiration arose from our small town's unexpected muses. His wife left plates heaped with buttery blueberry pancakes and plump sausages wrapped in foil knowing I subsisted haphazardly on cereal and fruit when deadlines were upon me.

Their quiet kindness manifested through thoughtfulness and crafted objects echoed generations nurturing this community's creative spirit from quilting circles to amateur theatricals showcasing local talents. Even the doctor's office displayed my sister's bold abstract oils rather than stale pharmaceutical adverts. No wonder I felt so anchored in my roots despite chasing inspiration across creative landscapes foreign to this rural township.

Out in my studio, I gazed affectionately over the jumble of projects in process, easels sporting acrylic experiments and half-sanded woodcut prints drying unevenly after late night printmaking marathons with Lily. Photos of her twin boys Finn and Tanner making silly faces with paint smeared joyfully across their chubby toddler cheeks never failed to bring bittersweet smiles. How quickly youthful abandon transforms before crushing self-consciousness and peer pressure dims the light in children's' eyes. Yet resilience also blooms when loving support builds up those dreams through their failures and doubts.

Not that Lily, now mother of two active boys and wife to her high school sweetheart, Brad, the building contractor, accepted limitations on possible futures. We both inherited our Irish mother's stubborn tenacity towards advocating passions deemed impractical. Thankfully after years of worry about his daughters abandoning stable careers to risk unreliable artistic livelihoods, we watched our stoic father frame award ribbons and enthusiastic local newspaper reviews of our burgeoning success.

I finished a commissioned painting of a country scene for Mrs. Abbott's upcoming gallery exhibition. With my brush I thoughtfully transformed angular shapes into lyrical, flowing abstraction across the canvas. As I painted, I channeled the inspiration of past generations. Those who hunched over sturdy plow handles in frostbitten mornings, or slowly whittled handmade toys during long winter nights beside the fire. Their collective community spirit endured, embodied in their everyday functional craftsmanship and infusing a sense of meaning into each small creative act with care and focus.

I felt this ancestral connection to creative spirit as I became mesmerized by small moments of shifting daylight or dancing dust in my paint-stippled studio. My greatest hope was to capture the transient yet deeply human essence of those passing magical instants most overlook in their busy routines. As I layered delicate color washes and sweeping charcoal shadows onto stark white, hopefully transcending mundane sight into revealed truth and beauty.

In this way, the hours slipped away as though I too joined those firefly glimpses shimmering bright with significance before winking mysteriously into the infinite cosmos. At day's end with a restful smile, I tidied paint bottles and stray brushes as our community's enduring gift pulsed on within me.

I looked around my paint-speckled studio. Making art isn't a 9 to 5 job - inspiration hits randomly without schedule. Chasing that fleeting spark meant having a flexible, curious spirit. My painting clothes were splattered with blue paint but I didn't mind the mess. Spilling paint was just part of the process of creating meaningful works.

I felt proud of the chaotic workspace overflowing with visions not yet realized. But sharing my private dreams still felt scary at times. I wondered - what breathtaking art might yet spill out from ordinary people's imaginations if their dull routines made them forget creativity simmering inside? What hidden talents await unlocking?

As the last hues of the sunset bled into the dusky twilight, a familiar restlessness took hold of me, a longing for something more, something tangible beyond the ephemeral dance of light and shadow on canvas. My thoughts drifted again to the upcoming art show at Mrs. Abbott's gallery, a beacon of culture and creativity in our small town.

The gallery, with its prime location at the heart of Main Street, had always been more than just a building to me. It stood as a testament to the town's vibrant artistic pulse, a place where local talent met the curious eyes of townspeople and tourists alike. Its wonderful ambiance, from the warmly lit display windows to the inviting open door, seemed to beckon passersby to step inside, to lose themselves in the world of colors and forms.

As I thought about my pieces adorning the aged walls, a sense of pride swelled within me. The gallery had provided a platform not just for me, but for many local artists, to share our inner worlds with the community. The thought of the upcoming show sent a ripple of excitement through me. It was an opportunity to connect, to communicate without words, to be seen.

And yet, beneath the anticipation, there lay a deeper, more persistent dream. I had always harbored the desire to one day own the gallery. This wasn't born out of a mere wish for possession, but from a profound connection to this space that had given so much to me and to others. I envisioned transforming it further, making it even more welcoming, more inclusive, a hub of creativity and learning that could inspire the next generation just as I had been inspired.

The gallery, with its perfect blend of location, ambiance, and history, was the heart of our artistic community. It was where the vibrant energy of the town's culture was most alive, where locals and tourists alike converged to witness the fruits of our collective imagination. The thought of being at the helm, guiding it towards an even brighter future, filled me with a purpose I hadn't fully acknowledged until now.

In my mind's eye, I saw the gallery not just as a venue for art, but as a sanctuary for the creative soul, a place where young and old could come to discover, learn, and express. I imagined art classes for children, painting the same sea glass and driftwood that had fascinated me as a child, and evenings where the community could gather to discuss art, history, and dreams.

But these were thoughts for another time. Tonight, I had the bar's familiar camaraderie awaiting me, a different but equally cherished part of my life's tapestry. Yet as I locked the studio door behind me, the gallery's image lingered in my mind, a symbol of what could be, a dream that maybe, just maybe, was within reach.

When the AfterShock Bar's smudged windows came into view, I hesitated remembering familiar faces likely gathered inside just as endless weekends prior. Boisterous laughter and clinking pint glasses scored old Bon Jovi songs screeching from the corner jukebox. Regulars tossed darts while trading jokes near taxidermy deer heads watching silently for generations. My high school friend Jenna would be pouring drinks, her ponytail swaying to Def Leopard's pounding drums while she laughed over patrons' outrageous stories. Even air heavy from decades of cigarette smoke and beer funk offered continuity like Grammy's patchouli perfume lingering in woolen hugs.

As I stepped into the dim warmth of AfterShock Bar, the familiar cocoon of laughter and clinking glasses wrapped around me like a well-worn quilt. It was a comfort, a routine, a scene painted over the canvas of my life with the steady hand of repetition. Yet, tonight, beneath the surface of that warmth, a current of restlessness stirred within me, like the first unpredictable strokes on a blank canvas that could disrupt the balance of a well-thought composition.

My eyes, adjusting to the bar's shadowed corners, instinctively scanned the room, acknowledging the regulars, the fixtures of my life's backdrop. Then, he caught my eye—a stark contrast to the familiar tableau, a disruption to the pattern I knew so well. His presence was like a bold color splashed unexpectedly across a monochrome sketch, drawing the eye, compelling and unanticipated.

His gaze met mine, and for a moment, the world seemed to tilt on its axis. It was as if he saw past the facade of the local artist, the girl with paint under her nails and dreams tucked away in the corners of her worn sketchbooks. In his eyes, there was a depth of understanding, a recognition of the aspirations and fears that I had whispered only to the night. It was both thrilling and terrifying, this feeling of being truly seen, not just looked at.

My heart raced, not just from the novelty of the encounter, but from the sudden awakening of long-dormant dreams and desires. Here was someone who had traversed worlds beyond the familiar streets of our town, who carried with him stories of places I had only dared to sketch in the quiet hours of dawn. The possibility of sharing those experiences, of painting his stories onto the canvas of my art, ignited a spark of longing I hadn't realized I'd been suppressing.

Yet, with the excitement came a tide of doubt. Was I ready to step beyond the comfort of my small but satisfying world? To risk the safety of my routine for the uncertainty of new horizons? The thought of altering the delicate balance of my life for an unknown future was as daunting as staring at a blank canvas, brush poised but hesitant to mar its pristine surface.

As we held each other's gaze, a silent conversation unfolded between us. Questions without words, answers felt rather than spoken. It was a moment suspended in time, a breath held before the plunge. I saw in him a mirror to my own restless spirit, a kindred searcher for meaning beyond the boundaries of our small town existence.

I hurried outside, propelled by a force I couldn't name. The night air, cool against my flushed cheeks, felt like a splash of cold water, snapping me out of the trance. The familiar landscape of the town, bathed in the ethereal glow of the moon, suddenly whispered promises of adventure and discovery. It was as if, in that brief encounter, he had painted over my world in new hues, revealing hidden depths I had yet to explore.

My pulse thrummed with a mix of fear and anticipation. For years, I had cocooned myself in the safety of the known, the comfortable. But now, the prospect of venturing into the unknown, guided by the hand of someone who had seen the world, filled me with a sense of purpose I hadn't felt in years. It was a leap of faith, a step into the void, but for the first time, I felt ready to embrace the uncertainty, to let it shape me, to allow my art—and my heart—to evolve in ways I had never dared imagine.

Tonight, the ordinary had been transformed into the extraordinary. The same old streets beckoned with new paths, and I stood at the crossroads, my destiny no longer a series of cautious brushstrokes, but a bold, sweeping arc, daring and unconfined. As I looked up at the stars, now shimmering with possibilities, I knew nothing would be the same. I had been awakened, not just to the potential of new worlds beyond, but to the unexplored landscapes within myself.

Echoes and Awakenings

Shane

I spent Saturday morning tidying up the cottage, reacquainting myself with the beloved space. Dusting Gramma's porcelain knickknacks and Granddad's well-worn carpentry tools suited me perfectly after chaotic months overseas. The mundane domestic motions anchored me while warm sunlight slanted through gingham curtains, keeping me company as I scrubbed away silent cobwebs. By late afternoon, the old floors gleamed invitingly again as I hauled trash bags stuffed with musty moth-eaten afghans out back.

I washed up as the summer evening cooled then sauntered downhill feeling lighter than I had in ages. Despite sore muscles from long-neglected chores, I inhaled deep gulps of fresh air untainted by stench of war. My combat boots hit Main Street's cracked pavement, instinct steering me towards the AfterShock Bar & Grill's garish flashing beer signs. Raucous laughter and smoky camaraderie called after too many nights peering into darkness anticipating demons. I hoped some of my old high school friends, now grown, might be tossing darts and talking up the waitresses' assets as usual.

My eyes were just adjusting to the dive's dimness when a meaty paw clapped my shoulder, nearly earning its owner a crotch full of my Ka-Bar knife. "Well slap me sober, if it ain't Shane Cooper hisself! Heard you were back in town!" Duke's ruddy face peered at me, bushy beard not fully disguising his shit-eating grin. "Damn boy, combat got you strung tighter than Mama June in a corset!"

I clasped his hand, thumping his back. "And I see you're still sauced earlier than a brine-soaked Thanksgiving bird. Some things never change, ya old coot." My smile likely looked more jagged relief than amusement at the near friendly fire. I waved over Duke's other paunchy childhood friends crowding the warped bar as 80's southern rock jangled the outdated Wurlitzer. Cigarette smoke eddied with stale bar perfume and unwashed clothes souring the windowless room. Just like high school minus twenty years seasoning small town ennui.

I let Duke press an icy can into my hand; not necessarily an old favorite but after MRE's and desert cistern sludge, free domestic beer equaled ambrosia. We jockeyed for elbow room among faded license plates and deer skulls lacquered dark with decades of nicotine dripping haphazardly across knotty pine. Jimmy tilted his foam mug in greeting, graying scruff matching the well-loved Carharrts identifying him as third generation mill worker. Beside him Big Frankie dwarfed the barstools, perpetually clad in his dad's mechanic shop shirts although we all knew he pumped septic systems for a living. Not glamorous perhaps, but vital as arteries everywhere keep life flowing, no matter what clots try blocking freedom's pulse.

We caught up over peanuts and shots, laughing too loudly replaying glory days pranks until tears streamed. Stories drifted towards embellished sexcapades – Duke boasted boning the entire 1992 prom court in his dad's hot-tub, while Frankie one-upped him screwing triplets during Shore leave. Testosterone and white lies fueled outlandish memories, nudging trauma's lingering shadows aside.

As my old friends told me about what had happened around town since I'd been gone, I mostly just listened. They shared news about people we grew up with - the divorces, diseases, and even drug overdoses becoming all too common. Our hometown may seem quaint on the outside, but tragedy still strikes too often behind white picket fences. It saddened me realizing everyone faces some darkness, no matter where life takes you.

The guys joked about old high school girlfriends who suddenly married in haste and had kids, like trying to stave off fears about fading looks and wasting potential. I suppose it's human nature to grasp for meaning through family when the future seems scary and uncertain approaching middle age. Predictable, I guess, but depressing to witness people abandoning their dreams because they numb themselves to passion and growth along the way.

I recounted a few colorful stories of my own about military missions abroad for gunrunners and explosives. Eyes widened hearing firsthand accounts from the front lines - probably pretty exotic compared to automobile plant layoffs and high school football glory days long gone. My tales offered excitement and escape during lulls in conversation. And in return, connecting with these long-time buddies re-anchored me in the bedrock of childhood nostalgia that shaped my early identity. I regained bearings once solid but now wavering after too much time adrift.

We were debating getting another round when the creaky wooden door swung open. In wandered a willowy chestnut-haired woman I faintly recognized but couldn't place. Her vintage Fleetwood Mac shirt and dusty boots sparked hazy memories under the dim neon lights. She glided easily past the faded welcome mat like she belonged here, though lacked the garish makeup or skin-tight outfits of the usual female patrons.

"Oh hey, it's Emily Sinclair," Duke exclaimed, snapping his fingers. "Sam's kid. Teaches art lessons to bratty tourists in the summer." Murmurs of recognition rippled through our cluster as I studied her anew. Emily Sinclair...four years below me in high school. The mousy freshman who ghosted through corridors leaving stray pencil sketches swirling in her wake. The girl I had seen yesterday, who had vanished like Cinderella leaving the ball.

Now in the sultry glow of beer signs, glimpses emerged of the waif-like wallflower. Willowy limbs elongated from gangly adolescence, skimming cutoffs hinting alluringly of smooth skin begging exploration. Loose waves of chestnut hair swept slender shoulders, making me itch to sweep it aside and graze lips along her exposed neck. While feeding the jukebox, she casually twisted those silken tresses into a knot, igniting an unexpected appetite.

As Emily floated towards the back office on some unhurried errand, faded memories collided abruptly with unexpected carnal hunger. Gone was the wide-eyed artsy kid habitually cloaked in oversized hoodies and rainbow tufts. In her place, an unfathomable allure stirred by this casually confident woman who moved through our hangout with subtle sensuality hitting me squarely in the chest. I shifted on worn vinyl, realizing Emily Sinclair posed an intriguing collision of past innocence and simmering mystery unexpectedly ignited by simple familiarity upended.

TIDES OF DESIRE A SOLDIER'S CANVAS

I watched her smile widen reading some yellowed band sticker, nose crinkling delightfully. Then suddenly our eyes caught across the smoky void and locked for a humid heartbeat. Soft recognition lit her autumn gaze with undisguised curiosity sparking connection. My mouth went dry struck by intuition of possibility glowing unexpectedly vivid. In that split second I sensed her seeing beyond bravado to a private longing. No judgment, just openness accepting people's multifaceted soul songs wordlessly.

And like any good Marine, once I identify strategic treasure, my mission becomes acquiring the prize against all obstacles. The target lodestone in Emily's bemused eyes eclipsed the entire bar's existence in an instant. I nearly stood to intersect her path outside when she unexpectedly turned away, hurrying out empty-handed. Disappointment twisted strangely as her silhouette receded then disappeared. I shook off impatient friends' teasing about "getting all moon-eyed over Sinclair's funny daughter" and swallowed the beer's bitterness. Our garish laughter resumed belatedly when Lynard Skynard's opening twang ripped over scintillating absence.

As twilight melted into the deep blue of the night, I found myself wandering the familiar streets of my hometown. Each step felt like a testament to the storm of emotions churning inside me. The city, with its old-world charm seamlessly blending into subtle modern nuances, seemed to echo my inner conflict. The shop fronts that hadn't changed since my childhood, the cobblestone paths worn smooth by countless footsteps before mine, and the gentle illumination from the street lamps casting long, thoughtful shadows—all spoke of a past life, a life before the chaos of war had redefined what normal meant to me.

Passing by the closed doors of Main Street, I couldn't help but feel the stark contrast between the city's beauty under the soft dawn light and the darkness that had found a home within me. The architectural grace of these buildings, mixing Victorian elegance with brick-clad storefronts, told stories of resilience and history that mirrored my own. Yet, they also highlighted the gap between who I was and who I wished to be.

This city, with its peaceful parks and the quiet flow of the Ocmulgee River, had always been a backdrop to my younger self's dreams. Now, it felt more like a mirror, reflecting my search for peace and the simplicity I longed for amidst the turmoil that had become my shadow.

My mind wandered to Emily Sinclair, who seemed to personify the city's understated beauty and its artistic heartbeat. Her unexpected presence had sparked something within me that had lain dormant for too long—hope, perhaps, or the flicker of a dream I thought I had left behind. Emily, with her hands marked by paint and her eyes shining with creativity, seemed to capture the essence of this place—unassuming yet full of life, familiar yet enshrouded in mystery.

As I made my way toward the riverwalk, the city unfolded beside me. The old stone bridges and the reflective waters of the river were silent companions to my thoughts. The city's beauty at night, bathed in the moon's soft glow and the twinkle of stars, offered a brief escape from the demons that haunted me. It was here, among the quiet harmony of nature and urban elegance, that I felt the first real stirrings of connection, deeper than any I had known before.

The journey I found myself on—wrestling with reintegration, seeking out my identity, and the pursuit of something resembling peace—was mirrored in the timeless beauty around me. The city stood as a beacon of hope, a gentle reminder that even amidst scars and stories of the past, beauty and grace remained. Like me, the city bore the marks of time and history but refused to be defined solely by them.

In this moment of reflection, I realized that my path to healing might just intertwine with the city's quiet allure and Emily's resilient spirit. Maybe, in the creativity it sparked in souls like hers, I could find a way to piece together my fragmented self. The city, whispering tales of yesterday while promising a vibrant tomorrow, held the key to the peace I so desperately sought.

Making my way through the quiet streets as dawn began to break, painting the city in golds and ambers, I understood that the battle ahead wasn't about reclaiming the person I was before the war. It was about accepting the man I had become, embracing my scars, and finding my place in the rich tapestry of this city, and perhaps, alongside Emily. The road ahead wouldn't be easy, but as the city stirred to life around me, I felt a sense of purpose and belonging that had eluded me for too long.

Whispers of the Heart

Emily

I pulled up to my sister Lily's brick ranch-style home, parking crookedly behind the long line of cars crammed along the narrow street. Popping open the truck's creaky door, I hefted out my canvas tote bag, laden with shower gifts and a grocery bag of wine bottles clinking together. Humid air tinged with the sweetness of Lily's overflowing peony bushes swept over me as I shuffled up her front walk, frazzled strands of hair sticking to the sheen of sweat on my forehead. I paused on the Welcome Friends! door mat, taking a bracing inhale before plunging into bridal shower chaos.

The moment I edged open the door, squeals and laughter tumbled out along with my nephews swarming around my legs. "Auntie Em! Auntie Em!" the twins Tanner and Finn chorus, smearing frosting handprints onto my shorts as they hugged me fiercely. My eldest nephew Kyle grinned shyly behind them, lanky preteen frame ducking his shaggy mop out of sight. My sister Elaine's bubbly voice rose above the din of wine-fueled female chatter: "Emily! Where have you been hiding yourself, sister dear?"

I flushed as a dozen neighborhood wives, cousins, and old high school friends suddenly flocked my way, cooing welcomes and plying me with pink rosé punch. Lily shot me a wry smile as she untangled herself from the gaggle, flaming red hair frizzier than usual as she blew stray curls off her forehead.

"Come on in, Em, sorry about the 3-ring circus today! Samantha's about to open gifts in the living room."

Squeezing my hand affectionately, Lily helped wrestle my overstuffed tote from my moist grip, handing it off to Elaine to stash under the dessert table. A tide of Estee Lauder perfume and swishing linen sundresses carried me towards the burst of laughter as Samantha, the bubbly bride to be, held up an enormous sparkling penis jewelry box. "Well Michael sure knows the key to THIS honeymoon vehicle!" She winked, the whole room collapsing into giggles as I settled cross-legged onto an ottoman. Lily pressed a fresh glass of sangria into my palm with a whispered "hair of the dog?" waggle of her eyebrows, knowing me too well.

As Sophia, Lily's neighbor, passed the glittering ring box around for closer inspection, I felt myself tuning out Samantha squealing over edible underwear favors, suddenly lost in my own thoughts. The sangria's icy sweetness turned acrid on my tongue as I replayed last night's electric moment seeing the handsome man at the dive bar.

Last night I learned the man's name who made my heart race with just one soul-reaching look. Shane. His eyes burned into mine even as I hid shy in the dark corner of the bar. Now here in blinding daylight at my sister's friend's wedding shower, I kept imagining Shane's handsome face. His intense gaze stuck in my head like a ghost floating at the edge of my vision. I'd get all distracted from chit chat and cake tasting when snippets of last night replayed.

The way quiet sadness and strength shone from Shane's eyes in smoky shadows. My cheeks would get hot reliving how breathless his stare left me. I'd snap back to giggles and girls toasting the glowing bride with champagne. But phantom Shane still pulled at me while I sat there among feminine ruffles and perfume. That rugged man had awoken some dormant longing in me with just one exchanged glance. And I knew these bachelorette festivities couldn't eclipse the tempting awareness kindled unexpectedly the night before.

Something about his stalwart confidence belying those soulful eyes had resurrected long-buried memories from high school hallways of a familiar broad-shouldered profile. I blinked at the merlot sloshing dangerously close to Aunt Clara's hand-crocheted linen doily as I struggled placing why Shane seemed familiar beyond our silent but startling connection last night. Then I gasped audibly, my wine glass dropping with a slosh as I made the high school math suddenly click.

"Em honey, you okay over there?" Lily touched my shoulder, her forehead crumpled with concern noticing what must be impossibly widened eyes fixed blindly at a cheese ball tower base. I nodded mutely as scenes from adolescence filtered abruptly into clarity.

Shane Cooper. The strong silent heartthrob type who moved with understated power through the halls, sending every girl swooning behind their American History textbooks. And who starred in way more of my own English Lit essay daydreams than I ever let be known beyond crumpled notebook margins.

"You look like you've seen a ghost, sweetie!" My mother's gentle lilt at my elbow finally broke the flashback spell, sucking me back to bridal white tulle and frosted champagne toasting all around. I smiled weakly, stammering some lame excuse about low blood sugar while my thoughts raced recklessly. Shane Cooper had returned home, a battle-worn soldier, now stirring once-secret longings I thought I had grown past.

His searching gaze last night revealed wounds and mysteries haunting the boyish golden child who graduated top of our class then shipped overseas before commencement caps hit the grass. Did his steadfast honor and courage still shine somewhere behind that stoic marine façade? If fate brought us together again, would the man find me a frivolous folly compared to lovers he left scattered across continents thanks to lonely tours of duty?

"Earth to Auntie Em!" I startled back again to find the twins tugging my limp palms towards a snaking Conga line led by Samantha shaking her glittery bust happily. Lily plopped a grape crown atop my messy waves, giggling as she tugged me to my unsteady feet. "Tell us where your head's at, baby sis! You've been spaced out all afternoon." Behind her beaming grin I glimpsed worry pinching her strong Irish cheekbones so reminiscent of our mother, Maeve.

At the bridal shower, amidst laughter and clinking glasses, I remember that fleeting glimpse of Shane from across the room. That brief moment unleashes a tide of desire, leaving me breathless. His presence was unexpected, a vibrant streak across my steady sky, and just as quickly, I'm swept up in a whirlwind of what-ifs and maybes.

But as quickly as the excitement surges, a shadow of doubt trails behind it. His life, bound to the military's unpredictable call, stands in stark contrast to my search for stability. How can I allow myself this fantasy when reality whispers that he could vanish just as swiftly as he appeared?

That single glance across the crowded room has unsettled me, splashing paint on a mural of longing and uncertainty. Can I truly open my heart to someone who walks a path so fraught with absence and risk? Amidst the festivity, I find myself adrift, caught between the allure of a possible love and the fear of a solitary goodbye.

Under the Summer Stars

Shane

I had been home for a few weeks now, each day blending into the next with a routine that was both comforting and monotonous. The area of Wesleyan Woods, with its familiar faces and unchanged landscapes, offered a sense of stability I craved after years of chaos. Yet, beneath the tranquility, a restlessness stirred—a longing for something, or someone, that could ignite a spark in my settled existence.

On a day that began like any other, I decided to break from my routine and visit the local art gallery hosting a summer exhibition. It was a small event, but it promised a change of scenery and a momentary escape from the solitude of my grandparents' cottage.

Walking into that art gallery, I figured it'd just be another boring afternoon to get through. I wasn't really an artsy kind of guy - give me a good action movie or a cold beer with buddies over some painting of a bowl of fruit any day. But I have to admit, those colorful pictures drew me in with their emotion. Made me feel not so numb inside for once as my eyes wandered over the vivid blues, fiery reds, peaceful greens.

And that's when I saw her again across the room - Emily. The pretty girl from the run-down bar with the sad eyes but contagious laugh. Instantly my heart raced just like that first chance meeting a while back. Our eyes met from across the museum-quiet hall and I swear everything else blurred away except her. Like we were the only two people still left in the world standing there.

Emily looked just as surprised to see me, but her sweet face lit up with a smile that hit me right in the gut. I walked towards her without even meaning to, like we were opposite ends of strong magnets pulled helplessly together. Up close again I noticed little details about her I missed in the dive bar shadows - flecks of orange paint and glitter dusting her face, ink stains across her paint-splattered jeans, tiny wildflower-shaped earrings shining against all that chestnut hair spilling loose around slight shoulders. An intoxicating scent of summer nights and vanilla clinging to her skin.

We exchanged nervous pleasantries about the gallery at first, both suddenly shy now together unchaperoned without beers or art patrons surrounding us. Didn't take long before our chatter got personal. I told her about losing my squad overseas, the survivor's guilt that shadowed my homecoming still. She asked thoughtful questions - not pitying exactly but showing she genuinely cared to understand better. I found myself confessing private doubts and fears about life's meaning post-war that I rarely voiced aloud even to myself.

It just felt...safe somehow opening up to Emily like I hadn't been able to with anybody else yet. Not old high school buddies or rowdy Marines determined to rekindle adolescent recklessness even off-duty. She wasn't judging anything I said or trying to change my perspective to feel less grim. She patiently just listened closely with those kind green eyes that seemed lit from within with empathy. I realized I craved just being truly seen and accepted exactly as is rather than measured constantly against absurd macho standards.

In turn Emily confided in me about her artistic temperament feeling at odds with our bustling materialistic society. Her creative soul struggled trying to adapt to expected roles or crushing workload draining passion's joy too often. How in nature's quiet observation she found rescue from depression that nobody glimpsed beneath the carefree hippie-chick facade except maybe her sister. I admired Emily's courage leaving soul-crushing corporate graphic design behind and nurturing whimsical artistic talents closer aligned with her heart's desire.

As the evening unfolded, with the gallery's artwork setting a backdrop for our unexpected reunion, the conversation between Emily and me flowed more freely than I would have thought possible. It was during one of these exchanges, as we stood side by side admiring a particularly vibrant canvas, that Emily's laughter faded into a moment of vulnerability.

"You know," she began, her voice lower, tinged with a hesitance I hadn't heard from her before, "this is the first time in a long while I've let myself get this close to art again."

I turned to her, sensing the weight of her words. "How come?" I asked, genuinely curious about what could make someone as talented as Emily doubt her place in the world of art.

She sighed, a small frown creasing her brow as she traced the edge of the frame with a finger. "I had someone in my life, not too long ago, who didn't believe in my art. He made it clear he thought my work was... frivolous. That I'd never be good enough."

The pain in her voice struck a chord within me. Here was Emily, vibrant and full of life, yet carrying the scars of someone else's disregard for her passion. It made my blood boil to think of her creativity being stifled by someone else's inability to appreciate it.

"I'm sorry to hear that," I said, my words feeling inadequate to address the depth of hurt that must have caused her. "But for what it's worth, I think your art is incredible. It speaks in ways words can't."

Emily smiled, a little wistfully, but I saw the spark in her eyes reignite. "Thank you, Shane. It's been a journey, trying to find my way back to believing in myself and my art. Tonight, being here, talking to you... it feels like I'm finally moving in the right direction."

Her admission warmed me, filling me with an admiration for her resilience. "You're stronger than you know, Emily. And for the record, anyone who can't see the talent and emotion you pour into your work doesn't deserve a place in your life."

Her laughter returned, lighter this time, as if a weight had been lifted from her shoulders. "I'm beginning to see that now," she said, her gaze meeting mine with newfound determination. "And I'm done letting someone else's negativity dictate how I feel about my art."

As we continued our walk, the conversation shifted between laughter and more serious discussions, but a new undercurrent of understanding flowed between us. Emily's struggle with her past relationship and its impact on her art added a layer of complexity to her that made me admire her even more. Her courage in facing those demons, in choosing to believe in her worth and her talent despite the hurt, resonated deeply with me.

Our connection, already strong from shared experiences and mutual attraction, deepened further with this exchange. The realization that we both were battling our pasts to build a future that felt true to ourselves made the bond between us feel almost fated. As the night grew darker and the fireflies danced around us, I felt a profound sense of gratitude for this moment, for the chance to be here with Emily, sharing not just our dreams but also our fears and our hopes for healing.

The simple act of holding her hand as we meandered along the river felt like a silent vow to support each other, to be the strength the other needed to overcome the shadows of the past. In that moment, under the summer stars, I knew that whatever the future held, Emily and I had found something rare and beautiful in each other—a shared understanding and a mutual respect that went beyond the surface, touching the very core of who we were.

As the evening waned and the moment to part ways loomed inevitable, Emily and I found ourselves lingering on the brink of farewell, neither quite ready to sever the connection that had deepened with the night's confidences and shared laughter. The fireflies continued their dance around us, casting a soft glow that seemed to encapsulate the bubble we existed in, separate from the rest of the world.

I could feel the hesitation in both of us, a mutual reluctance to let go of the evening and step back into our separate lives. The air between us was charged with an intensity that hadn't been there at the start of the night, a tangible pull that seemed to draw us closer without conscious thought.

Finally, as if pulled by an unseen force, I stepped forward, closing the distance between us. Emily's eyes lifted to mine, wide and luminous in the dim light, reflecting a mix of emotions that mirrored my own. There was a question in her gaze, a silent inquiry that I answered by cupping her face gently in my hands, my thumbs brushing lightly over her cheeks.

The world seemed to hold its breath as I leaned down, my heart pounding with a mix of nerves and anticipation. Our lips met in a kiss that was both a promise and a discovery, gentle at first, but growing more insistent as if we were both seeking answers in the touch. Emily's hands found their way to my shoulders, clinging to me as if she could anchor herself in the storm of sensations that the kiss unleashed.

It was a kiss that spoke of possibilities, of the yearning for something more, yet also carried the unspoken agreement that now was not the time. Our realities, the complexities of our lives and pasts, hovered at the edges of this perfect moment, reminding us that patience was a virtue we both needed to embrace.

As we finally, reluctantly, broke apart, the world rushed back in with the cool night air, leaving us both breathless and acutely aware of the connection that had just been forged. Emily's face was flushed, her eyes bright with an emotion that made my heart skip a beat, and I knew I was wearing a similar expression.

"We should probably say goodnight," I murmured, my voice rough with the effort of pulling back from the edge of the precipice we'd found ourselves on.

"Yes, goodnight," Emily echoed, her voice soft but steady, laced with the promise of future explorations.

But in that moment of parting, with the taste of her still lingering on my lips, I knew that what we'd shared tonight was only the beginning. The kiss had been a door opened to a new possibility, a path neither of us could walk just yet, but one we both seemed eager to explore when the time was right.

We parted with a final, lingering look, a silent vow that this was not the end but merely a pause. As I walked Emily to her studio, I felt a stirring of hope mixed with the sweet ache of longing. Tonight had changed something fundamental between us, and I found myself looking forward to the day when we could explore the depths of what had sparked under the summer stars.

The drive back to my grandparents' cottage was a blur of emotion and replayed memories, the echo of Emily's laughter and the warmth of her hand in mine a constant presence in my mind. The night had ended, but the journey we'd embarked on was just beginning, and I was ready to see where it would lead us, together.

Blooms of the Heart

Emily

As Shane and I slowly made our way to my studio under the cover of the starlit sky, the euphoria from our kiss lingered, wrapping around me like a comforting embrace. Yet, beneath the surface of this newfound joy, a current of apprehension tugged relentlessly at my heart. The fear of Shane's inevitable departure at summer's end haunted the edges of my happiness, casting long shadows over the bright future I dared to envision with him.

The quiet of the night, with the chorus of crickets and the soft rustling of leaves, accentuated the reality of our situation. Shane was still a soldier, his duty bound to call him away, back to a world far removed from the tranquility of our small town and the intimate moments we shared in my studio. The thought of him leaving, of this magical bubble we existed in bursting, filled me with a dread I couldn't shake.

As we reached the doorstep of my studio, the place where my soul felt most alive and vulnerable, the warmth of Shane's hand in mine offered a stark contrast to the cold fear within me. I found myself grappling with the vulnerability that love had ushered in, a stark reminder of how much I had to lose. The memory of past heartache, of being deemed not enough, crept insidiously into my mind, fueling my fear that this, too, could end in pain.

Shane, sensing my sudden quietness, turned to face me, his eyes searching mine for clues to my sudden shift in mood. In his gaze, I found a well of understanding and patience, a silent reassurance that he was here, now, with me. But the specter of his departure loomed large, a barrier that seemed insurmountable despite our growing connection.

"Emily," Shane began, his voice gentle, breaking the silence that had enveloped us. "What's on your mind?"

The concern in his voice, so genuine and devoid of judgment, crumbled the last of my defenses. Standing there, in the shadow of my studio—the very embodiment of my dreams and vulnerabilities—I found the courage to voice my fears, to lay bare the vulnerability that love had unearthed.

"I'm scared," I confessed, the words barely a whisper against the backdrop of the night. "Scared of how much I'm starting to feel for you, and terrified of the moment you'll have to leave."

Shane's response was immediate, his hands coming up to cradle my face, ensuring I met his earnest gaze. "Emily, I won't pretend I know what the future holds or that I won't have to leave when the summer ends. But I want you to know, what I feel for you, what's happening between us—it's not just a summer fling to me. There's something more here. I know we've only just started, but, I don't know how to describe it. There's a connection with you I want to explore."

His words, spoken with such sincerity, offered a balm to the ache in my heart. Yet, the uncertainty of our situation lingered, a bitter reminder that our time together might have a looming expiration date.

"I want to believe there can be an 'us', Shane, more than anything," I replied, my voice laced with a mix of hope and fear. "But the thought of opening my heart, only to have it break when you leave, it's overwhelming."

Shane pulled me closer, wrapping me in an embrace that spoke of protection and promise. "Let's not let the fear of what might happen tomorrow rob us of the happiness we can have today," he whispered, his breath warm against my ear. "I'm here now, Emily, and I'm not going anywhere until I absolutely have to. And even then, it won't be the end for us, not if I have anything to say about it."

In Shane's arms, outside the place where my true self was laid bare in every brushstroke and sculpted form, I allowed myself a moment of hope, a fleeting belief that perhaps we could defy the odds. But as we parted ways, with promises to see each other again soon, the fear of the future remained, a silent specter at the back of my mind. Despite Shane's reassurances, the vulnerability of my heart remained, tender and exposed, caught between the desire to love freely and the instinct to guard against the pain of loss.

As I watched him walk away, his figure gradually swallowed by the night, I made a silent vow to cherish every moment we had, to let our burgeoning feelings for each other guide us through the uncertainty, and to face whatever the future held, together. Yet, the echo of the studio door closing behind me felt like a gentle reminder of the solitude that might once again be my only companion, should the summer's end take Shane away from me.

The kiss beneath the summer stars had changed everything. It was not just a meeting of lips, but of hearts and hopes, fears and dreams. And as we stepped into the light of the cottage, I knew that no matter what the future held, this moment, this kiss, would be the beacon that guided us through.

I smiled giddily remembering his tender insistence on waiting until I was "ready for the beast within" before getting intimate. Such restraint from a handsome Marine who was, I am sure, used to lovers throwing themselves shamelessly at his camouflaged bulges. Yet that sensitivity proved how, unlike the flashy showoffs I'd dated before, Shane saw beyond surfaces into vulnerable parts of the heart. Now anticipation of seeing him again consumed all my thoughts.

The next evening Shane appeared grinning at my door clutching wildflowers, the summer breeze tousling his cropped blonde hair. My breath caught admiring how dashing that olive green Henley hugged solid biceps and broad chest. Lord save me from jumping this polite suitor before dinner's done!

"For the loveliest artist ever to capture this weary soldier's battered heart," he proclaimed with exaggerated gallantry.

"Well, well, Shane Cooper playing the charming gentleman with flowers - you sure clean up nice!" I finally managed to tease back after I was briefly left speechless by his smooth line.

As I filled up the chipped vase on my counter to display Shane's gift, it hit me that no man had ever given me flowers before. Most guys probably figured a free-spirited artsy woman like me just wants hot romance or passion. But Shane's thoughtful little token showed me that he understands women crave occasional romantic gestures too, even us wild creative types.

Those flowers told me Shane grasped that I have hidden hopes and fears lurking under my fun, crazy personality. Like he sensed I still had some relationship demons from my past that made it hard to risk real intimacy again. But the sincere way Shane gazed at me with those flowers showed his determination to gently banish any ghosts still haunting my heart. His eyes seemed to promise he'd stick around patiently until I felt safe to be vulnerable sharing a future together.

We meandered for hours hand-in-hand along wooded backcountry lanes bordering my family's ancient rolling farmland as orange sunset faded to violet dusk. Cicada serenades and meadowlarks' melodies accented meaningful conversation. Childhood memories were shared under soaring hawk-patrolled skies.

I learned Shane tragically lost his parents very young, and was lovingly raised by his devoted grandparents. His gramma in particular doted on Shane as her only grandchild. Craving purpose, Shane had enlisted in the Marines after high school, with his grandparent's full support. They attended his graduation ceremony bursting with bittersweet pride for their grandson's courageous path. They had both died shortly after his enlistment.

Meanwhile I explained about growing up in a vibrantly eccentric household, the baby of three artsy sisters. Our loving mother was a free-spirited painter who encouraged self-expression and adventure. Our steadfast father built his construction business from the ground up, juggling big projects but never missing dance recitals or art shows.

My dramatic middle sister, Lily, in particular, took me under her paint-stained wing ever since I could hold a brush. Though I struggled finding my unique style, Lily urged me to embrace every artistic whim without fearing mistakes. Thanks to my family's enthusiastic nurturing, I persevered through the predictable angst of high school to channel emotions into poignant paintings of loneliness, identity, and adolescent dreams. My parents, bohemian big sisters, and loyal best friends accepted my blue hair, thrift shop style, and brooding poetry phases with good humor through those awkward years. Their loving support gave me confidence to pursue my unconventional artistic talents without pressure to fit some mainstream mold.

Shane gently squeezed my hands in understanding as I shared hidden painful parts of myself in the quiet twilight. Unlike past guys I dated who made me feel silly for getting brooding or deep, Shane took me seriously. As a tough soldier, he had seen darkness himself and didn't write off my swirling emotions.

He said it felt like mystical energy surrounded me - maybe from childhood scars or just my artistic spirit. Where others saw only a moody, quirky girl painting strange pictures, Shane saw resilience and creative beauty even after going through hard things.

As the summer dusk faded to night around us, we turned towards his grandparents cozy cottage, drawn to spend more time together by the fireplace that waited for us to light it up and spark new beginnings.

The following weeks blazed as bright as shooting stars streaking recklessly towards earth. Routines were forgotten as we carved out idyllic hidden moments and obligations be damned. We spent hours watching dragonflies dimple glossy pond surfaces after laying on blankets finding shapes in the clouds. Rainy afternoons found us curled up reading tattered paperbacks aloud to the sputtering crackle of vinyl records on Gramma's antique phonograph. Shared glances sparked hunger leading to steamy times in each other's arms.

I sketched constantly trying to capture emotions forever – his focused laughter coaxing garden seeds to sprout after years untended...arms corded taut hoisting heavy oak furniture from damp basements into bright sunshine, making the cozy cottage ours...peace smoothing Shane's perpetually grim facade when lazing back enjoying harmonica melodies at dusk. Quiet joy swelled completing the abandoned dwelling's rehabilitation alongside someone invested fully. Not just a wandering ghost occupying a dead man's easy chair out of a sense of lingering duty stunted since youth. Together we nurtured forgotten dreams into full flowering again.

Shane and I talked so openly - both healing from life's painful blows in different ways. Bit by bit truths came out, feeling safe and unrushed with each other. I asked caring questions about Shane's life as a Marine so far, wanting to truly know the man under the confident facade. What had he faced up to this point - the losses and costs of dangers asked of him. I could tell shadows lingered in those striking eyes each time he deflected mentions of the future. And my woman's intuition sensed heavy burdens on his spirit despite being honored already as a courageous warrior. So we continued linking arms and listening for hours - my creative dreams revived while Shane's warrior heart began mending through my affection. In the golden summer fields Shane's rigid shell cracked open just enough...to release old pain and shining hopes too long bottled up tight. Maybe, by fate, our tangled paths crossed just in time before autumn chilled such fragile possibility.

Shadows and Light

Shane

Several days had passed since the night of the kiss, a moment that had imprinted itself in my memory with vivid clarity. The world around me continued its usual rhythm, but I found myself adrift in a haze of emotion and newfound connection.

The morning sun had barely crept over the horizon when I spotted the envelope. Its edges were crisp against the worn doormat, an ominous contrast to the usual bills and flyers. The texture of the envelope was unnervingly smooth, almost sterile, as if it had been plucked from a world far removed from the warmth of human touch. I hesitated, my hand hovering above it, the dread in my gut building with each passing second.

Finally, mustering the courage, I picked it up. The weight of the paper felt disproportionate, heavy with the news it carried, as if the words inside were made of lead rather than ink. My fingers trembled slightly as I broke the seal, an action that seemed in that moment to be a betrayal of the hope I'd been clinging to—that maybe, just maybe, everyone I knew had made it home.

As I unfolded the letter, the cold, impersonal typeface assaulted my eyes, each letter a stark reminder of the bureaucracy behind the words. "We regret to inform you..." it began, and that clichéd phrase was enough to send a jolt through my heart. The room seemed to tilt slightly, the morning light too bright, too harsh against the dark news staining the page.

A tightness seized my chest, an oppressive squeeze that made it hard to draw a full breath. The half-eaten breakfast on my table suddenly appeared grotesque, my stomach churning at the sight. Food seemed trivial, tasteless, in the face of such loss. I pushed the plate away, my appetite vanquished by the reality the letter represented.

My hands shook, not just from the shock, but from a resurgence of all-too-familiar grief. Memories of laughter, of shared hardships and victories on foreign soil, flooded my mind, each one a sharp jab to my already aching heart. The finality of the letter, the unyielding truth it delivered, was overwhelming.

Needing to escape the suffocating confines of my kitchen, I decided to go for a walk. The walls felt too close, the air too still, as if the house itself was mourning. I needed space to breathe, to process the tidal wave of emotions crashing over me. The need for movement, for physical exertion to match the turmoil inside, propelled me out the door.

The early morning air was cool, a stark contrast to the turmoil burning within me. Each step was automatic, my mind barely registering the familiar streets of Macon as I walked. The letter's words echoed in my head, a relentless loop that fueled my brisk pace. The reality of my friend's death, of the danger we all faced and somehow believed we could evade, settled heavy in my soul.

This walk, aimless and yet driven by a need to outrun my thoughts, became a small act of defiance against the pain. The physical motion, the rhythmic pounding of my feet against the pavement, offered a temporary reprieve, a chance to gather the shattered pieces of my composure. But even as I moved, I knew there was no escaping the truth, no outpacing the grief. The letter had changed everything, and now I had to face a world that was suddenly one friend poorer, one hero less.

Later, walking through the bustling streets of downtown Macon, the community event enveloped me in a sensory painting that felt both alien and comforting. The late afternoon sun bathed the scene in a warm, golden light, casting long shadows that stretched across the pavement, a stark contrast to the shadows lingering in my own heart. The air was alive with the sounds of laughter and music, a lively melody played by a local band that filled the space between the chatter of families and friends.

The smells of the festival were intoxicating—the sweet aroma of cotton candy mixed with the smoky scent of barbecued meats and the rich, earthy smell of freshly brewed coffee from a nearby stand. Children darted between booths, their laughter a bright thread woven through the fabric of the event, their faces painted with swirls of color and joy. It was a picture of peace and community, so far removed from the stark realities of my recent past.

As I meandered through the crowd, my gaze was drawn to the art displays that lined the street. One booth in particular caught my attention, featuring paintings that depicted scenes of battle and sacrifice. The brush strokes were bold and chaotic, yet there was a haunting beauty in the chaos—a portrayal of resilience amidst turmoil. Another artist showcased sculptures that evoked a sense of peace, their smooth lines and gentle curves offering a silent counterpoint to the violence depicted nearby. These pieces resonated deeply, reflecting the tumult of emotions churning within me—the longing for peace, the weight of loss, and the search for meaning after the chaos of war.

Despite the vibrancy around me, a sense of disconnection tugged at my soul. The festival, a celebration of life and art, seemed to exist in a world apart from the one I had known. Here, battles were fought with creativity and expression, not with guns and grit. Yet, amidst this disconnect, there was a longing—a yearning for the normalcy and connection that this event represented.

It was in this whirlwind of thought and emotion that I spotted Emily. She stood like a beacon of light against the backdrop of the festival, her presence grounding me in the moment. Her booth displayed her art, each piece a window into her soul. The colors were vibrant, alive with passion and depth, and I found myself drawn into the stories she told through her work. Her talent was undeniable, each painting evidence of her dedication and vision.

As I approached her, my heart raced with a mixture of anticipation and anxiety. "Hey, Emily," I managed, my voice steadier than I felt.

Her smile, bright and welcoming, was like a ray of sunshine piercing through the clouds of my mind. "Shane, hi! I didn't expect to see you here," she replied, her voice weaving through the noise around us, a familiar melody in the cacophony of the festival.

Our conversation flowed effortlessly, a comfortable exchange that bridged the gap between her world of art and my world of military service. Emily's enthusiasm for her work was infectious, and I found myself captivated not just by her art, but by her—by the depth of her passion, the warmth of her spirit, and the resilience of her character.

As the festival's lively atmosphere buzzed around us, a sense of foreboding tightened in my chest. The moment had come to broach the subject that had been weighing heavily on me since I received the letter. The words felt like boulders at the back of my throat, hard to swallow, harder still to voice. I hesitated, glancing at Emily, whose face was alight with the vibrancy of the event and the warmth of our interaction. The fear that this news could drive a wedge between us, dull the light in her eyes, was paralyzing.

"Emily, I got some bad news this morning. A fellow Marine. The funeral is in a few days," I finally said, my voice a strained whisper against the backdrop of festivities. The words hung between us, stark and cold, an unwelcome intrusion into the bubble we had created.

I watched her closely, bracing for the shift in her demeanor, the possible retreat in her warmth. Emily's reaction was crucial, not just for the continuation of our evening but for the fragile thread of connection that had started to weave between us. Her face fell slightly, the smile fading into a look of concern and empathy that was immediate and genuine.

"I'm so sorry, Shane. That must be hard," she replied, her voice soft, laden with genuine sorrow for my loss.

The relief that washed over me was palpable, mingling with the grief that the mention of the funeral had dredged up anew. It was a complex cocktail of emotions—gratitude for her understanding, sadness for my friend's death, and a bittersweet acknowledgment that Emily's empathy was a temporary shelter from the storm of my grief.

Her hand found mine, a tangible connection amidst the swirl of my tumultuous thoughts. "It is," I admitted, allowing the vulnerability to seep into my words. "But tonight was a good break from all that. Thank you for sharing this with me."

Emily's smile returned, though more subdued, her eyes shining with a gentle warmth that spoke volumes. "I'm glad you were here. If you ever need someone to talk to, or just want to escape for a bit, I'm here," she offered, her words a lifeline in the sea of my turmoil.

The gratitude I felt in that moment was immense, a buoyant force against the pull of my sorrow. Emily's response, her willingness to stand beside me in this moment of pain, underscored the depth of the connection we were building. It was a poignant reminder that even in the midst of grief, there was room for new beginnings, for hope.

Guiding Emily back to her studio, the air between us was thick with unspoken emotions, a tangible echo of the feelings we had tentatively begun to explore. Our journey was marked by silence, but it was a comfortable quiet, filled with shared glances and the occasional brush of hands that spoke volumes more than words ever could.

Upon reaching her doorstep, the moment of parting loomed over us, charged with the promise of something more. It was Emily who broke the silence, her voice a soft invitation laced with vulnerability. "Would you like to come in?" she asked, her eyes searching mine for an answer.

Without hesitation, I stepped into the warm embrace of her studio, a space as inviting and complex as Emily herself. The door closed behind us, sealing away the outside world and the last remnants of uncertainty that had accompanied us on our walk.

We moved to her living room, a cozy area bathed in the soft glow of evening light filtering through the curtains. Taking a seat on the sofa, we were suddenly enveloped in a shared solitude that felt both exhilarating and comforting. Side by side, the distance between us diminished not just in space but in the walls we had built around our hearts.

As we settled into the silence, our conversation turned to looks and soft laughs, a prelude to the confession of our desires. It was in this intimate setting, surrounded by the artifacts of Emily's life and passions, that the space between us became charged with anticipation. Every glance, every touch, was laden with meaning, drawing us inexorably toward the moment when all barriers would fall away.

Gazing into Emily's eyes, I saw the tempest of emotions swirling within—the rapid rise and fall of her chest betraying her racing heart. A desire to lose myself in the depth of her gaze, where fear meets longing, overwhelmed me. I leaned in, and with a feather-light touch, our lips met. It was a kiss that spoke of unspoken promises and a hunger long denied. Her arms snaked around my neck, pulling me closer, deepening our connection. My hands cradled her face, the softness of her skin against my palms anchoring me in the moment. In that kiss, the world faded away, leaving only the electric current that danced between us. Reluctantly, my hands guided her face back, breaking our kiss. I searched her eyes, seeking permission, a silent question hanging between us. The answer, a spark of shared desire and trust, ignited my resolve. My fingers traced a path down her back, a promise in every touch, as I lifted her effortlessly. In that unspoken agreement, every step toward the bedroom felt like a step into a shared future. Cradling her in my arms, every step towards our sanctuary was laden with anticipation. The warmth of her body against mine, the soft whisper of her breath against my neck, and the tender weight of her trust in my arms enveloped us in a cocoon of intimacy. Her bedroom, once just a room, transformed into a haven for the promises whispered and the silent vows made in the sanctity of our embrace.

Building Foundations

Emily

The morning after our night together felt like waking from a dream I never wanted to end. Shane's presence in my studio, now intertwined with mine in such an intimate way, changed the air itself—making it lighter, yet somehow more electric. As we shared breakfast, the conversation flowed effortlessly, weaving in laughter and comfortable silences. It was in these moments I realized, Shane wasn't just a fleeting connection; he was becoming a part of my very foundation.

The decision to help Shane with his grandparents' house came naturally. The house, with its faded walls and creaky floors, was a tribute to a love that had weathered time—a love I found myself yearning to emulate with Shane. Each stroke of paint, each nail hammered in, wasn't just a step towards restoration; it was a symbol of us building something durable, together.

Working side by side, our relationship deepened beyond the physical. I saw the care Shane put into preserving his grandparents' legacy, and it mirrored the care he showed me. His stories of childhood summers spent here, his laughter echoing in the empty rooms, his dreams for the future—it all knit together, forming a tapestry of trust and affection that I hadn't known I was missing.

As the house began to take shape, so did our relationship. We were two people, each with our own scars, finding healing in the act of creation. Whether it was through the shared victories of a refurbished room or the quiet support in moments of frustration, every day added another layer to our bond.

I hadn't realized how much I needed someone to share not just the burdens but the joys of life until Shane. And as we stood together, looking at the progress we'd made, I knew that what we were building was far more significant than just a house. It was a home, a life, a future—ours.

One night, as the dusk wrapped around us, the space between Shane and me electrified with anticipation. Shane's touch was gentle as his hands cradled my face, his fingers threading through my hair, his gaze intense with emotion that mirrored my own escalating heartbeat. In his eyes, I saw the raw depth of feeling laid bare, a silent conversation between our souls.

The world receded until there was nothing but the connection pulsing between us. Shane's embrace, both tender and strong, pulled me closer, erasing any distance left. It was a moment that captured the essence of our journey together, a mix of longing and profound affection.

I reached out, my arms encircling Shane, pressing myself against him. When our lips met, it was a kiss that sealed promises and whispered of dreams, intensifying as our pent-up emotions spilled over. I stepped back and licked my lips. He took three steps toward me, grabbed my face in his hands and kissed me passionately.

The world exploded around me. I gripped his shirt and held on for dear life as the electricity shot through my body. I had unleashed the beast and was more than ready for what was to come.

He leaned his forehead against mine and gazed into my eyes. He didn't speak, his hands went down to my hips, and he picked me up. My legs instinctively went around him, and he carried me to the bedroom while still kissing me.

He pushed me against a wall, his hands and mouth exploring my body. He reached down into my top and pulled a breast out, his mouth finding my nipple.

I moaned; his warm mouth felt so good but when he included his tongue I nearly screamed. This was all I wanted and more!

His hands went down to my skirt and pulled it the rest of the way up my hips, then his fingers found my warm, dripping wet center, I leaned my head back and shuddered. His fingers entered me slowly, all the while his mouth was still working on my nipple. I moaned loudly as he pushed them in and out of me.

I ground my hips against him, my panties were soaked. I ran my palms down his back, loving the way his muscles moved under my hands.

His mouth found mine again. I kissed him back hungrily, wanting more.

His fingers left my center and I could feel him moving to pull his member out of his pants. I couldn't think of anything else but his hard shaft inside me.

Thunder sounded above us, and I heard his zipper go down. I pulled back from the kiss, and he looked into my eyes as he entered me.

I drew in a breath as he filled me.

He started to rock his hips. His balls slapped against my ass. I cried out in pleasure. He just rocked into me harder.

I called his name; he leaned his head down and kissed and sucked on my neck.

I let out a long, deep moan, his cock grew inside me. The sensations that were ripping through my body sped up and heightened.

His hands went under my ass, and he lifted me.

I wrapped my feet around his back as he moved. His thrusts were hard and fast.

The electricity between us was causing me to see stars. I kissed his neck and bit his shoulder. He growled and his pace sped up.

He pulled out abruptly and turned me around, my hands braced against the bed frame. He pushed my skirt up to my waist and positioned himself behind me.

I was so wet, I was dripping. He thrust into me hard, pausing just for a moment to let me adjust.

He moved his hands up my sides and gripped my breasts. I moaned and pushed back against him.

He continued to move his hands up my body until they found my hair. He pulled my head back; my hands left the bed and went to his arms.

He started to thrust in and out of me, my legs grew weak, and my breathing grew shallow.

His movements were steady and controlled. His mouth found my ear and he whispered, "Come for me, Emily."

"Hard and fast!" I cried. I was on the brink, my body shaking. He kissed my neck and moaned, sending me over the edge.

I screamed, my body shaking violently. He growled and pushed his cock in hard. As he grabbed my hips and started pumping me, filling me to his hilt each time, I was bucking with each thrust. My orgasms were one right after the other, I couldn't stop, didn't want to stop.

I collapsed against the bed. He pulled out gently. The sensation of him leaving my body was overwhelming. His hands caressed my bottom. I turned around and kissed him.

"I warned you about the beast within." He looked at me with concern in his eyes.

I put my arms around him and held him tightly. In that embrace, every unspoken word, every shared hardship, and every moment of separation fused into a promise of hope and passionate commitment. Clinging to each other, it felt as though together, we could overcome anything.

Parting was a rush of breathless wonder, a realization that this was merely the start. We had found in each other a completion, a daring hope neither of us had allowed ourselves to fully embrace before. Our hands, still clasped as silence enveloped us, spoke of an unbreakable bond and a love ready to face any future. So now our nights often ended wrapped safe in each other's scarred embrace as crickets and a lone owl spoke beyond paned windows where we lay. With fingertips gently tracing the small scar left on his face by the Taliban, I wondered if anyone had truly witnessed the unwavering heart beating beneath all the medals and memorial ceremonies. Did the bereaved families whose sons Shane carried across the desert sands crying for emergency airlift comprehend the scars that are there, but unseen?

So carefree days continued, one into another as Shane helped rehabilitate the sagging wood cottage from drab abandoned relic back into cozy home reflecting us, two flawed yet hopeful souls writing fresh history within its periwinkle walls. We made memories while learning Gramma's famous blackberry cobbler recipe while Motown played...staining salvaged planks recovered from forgotten barn lofts into cozy bookshelves filled with childhood well-worn favorites. Hot hungry mouths exploring pleasure now that the beast had been unleashed as new lovers navigated uncharted passion.

Each mundane task was purposeful even though we knew our time was short. Our hidden bubble wouldn't allow harsh realities beyond summer's waning horizon. While thunder sometimes rumbled, reminding us of the inevitable parting as Shane's warrior calling summoned him away, we just lived and loved for the now, with hopes for a future together.

The Farewell

Shane

The sun dipped low, casting a soft glow over the Ocmulgee River, a melancholy light, reflecting the bittersweet culmination of our shared summer. Emily's hand in mine, once a source of boundless comfort, now felt like a poignant reminder of the impending separation. Our silent walks had become a ritual, each step a testament to a love that had blossomed unexpectedly but fiercely. The knowledge of my imminent return to Camp LeJeune hung over us, an unspoken dread that clouded our final days together. Our journey had been a whirlwind of emotion and discovery, each day a treasure I was reluctant to part with. Yet, as a soldier, duty called with a voice impossible to ignore. The intimate nights, the shared secrets, the laughter that filled our moments – they were becoming memories before their time.

I turned to her, the fading light reflecting in her eyes, showing a vulnerability I had never seen. "This isn't goodbye," I said, my voice heavy with unspoken fears. "It's a promise to return." The words felt inadequate, but they carried the weight of my commitment.

Her smile was bittersweet, a silent witness to the strength she wielded. "I know, Shane. It's just hard, knowing you'll be so far away." This was a new frontier for us, uncharted territory filled with unknowns. Our farewells had always been brief; never had the shadow of separation loomed so large.

Holding her close, I tried to memorize everything about her, hoping it would sustain me through the coming months. "I'll come back to you," I whispered, a vow to both her and myself.

Walking back into Camp LeJeune felt like moving through a parallel universe where everything had shifted slightly off-kilter. The barracks, once a haven of camaraderie and routine, now seemed like a hollow shell, echoing with the absence of Emily's laughter.

Martinez clapped me on the back with his usual vigor, pulling me back to a reality I wanted to escape. "Look who's back from dreamland," he jeered, though not unkindly. I mustered a grin, but it felt like stretching a muscle I hadn't used in ages.

The base's relentless rhythm pulls me from the grip of my memories. I wake before dawn, the barracks buzzing with the low hum of activity as soldiers ready themselves for the day. The clank of dog tags mixes with the muffled sounds of boots hitting the floor, a stark contrast to the quiet mornings I'd grown accustomed to, where the only sound was Emily's gentle breathing.

Training grounds become my world again, where orders are barked like a harsh dialect I had to reacquaint myself with. The physical exertion is a welcome distraction, yet each bead of sweat on my brow is a reminder of sunnier, softer days spent away from this rigor.

In the mess hall, the guys threw questions at me like grenades, each one exploding into memories I wanted to keep sacred, untainted by this place's sterile air. I dodged them with practiced ease, serving up sanitized versions of my time away, all the while feeling like a traitor to the vivid, aching beauty of my days with Emily.

In the evenings, the barracks are alive with the sounds of camaraderie and escapism: cards shuffling, dice rolling, and the occasional strum of a guitar. I try to immerse myself, to be one of the guys, but my heart strains against the invisible chain pulling me back to Emily.

Each night, as I lie in my bunk staring at the ceiling, the base's constant hum becomes a lullaby of duty and dedication. Yet, in the quiet of my heart, a counter-melody of longing and promise plays—a reminder of what I've left behind and what I'm fighting to return to.

The march to the commander's office felt longer than usual, every step echoing the weight of uncertainty. Inside, the air was stiff with formality, a stark contrast to the freedom of my recent days. The commander's face was a mask of professionalism, his eyes revealing nothing of the news he was about to deliver.

The commander laid out the mission with clinical precision, his voice steady, but I could sense the undercurrent of urgency. "Shane, at 0600 hours, our Black Hawk sent out a mayday. It went down in enemy territory. We've lost all comms. Satellite has the crash site, but our guys are out there alone, possibly injured. You need to get them out."

Maps sprawled across the table, lines and markers denoting enemy activity, potential hazards, and our insertion point. The weight of the upcoming mission, the lives at stake, pressed down on me. This wasn't just about following orders; it was a race against time in hostile territory, a test of everything I'd been trained to do.

I could feel the walls of the office closing in, a tangible reminder of the world I was bound to by duty. My mind raced, thoughts of Emily clashing with the reality of my soldier's oath. The promise I made to return to her felt like a fragile thread in the face of this new mission. Yet, as the details of the operation unfolded, my training kicked in, compartmentalizing my personal anguish, transforming it into the resolve I would need to lead my team.

Outside, the base continued its relentless pace, oblivious to the storm raging inside me. I walked back to my quarters in a daze, the weight of leadership and love pressing down on me. This was the life I had chosen, a life of service and sacrifice. But as I prepared for the mission ahead, my thoughts lingered on Emily, on the promises made in softer, quieter times, and on the world I hoped to return to. A determination settled over me, cold and hard. I was ready.

***

The weight of the mission sat heavy on my shoulders as I faced my team. The room, usually filled with banter and laughter, was now tense with anticipation. I could see it in their eyes – the resolve, the fear, the unspoken questions. This wasn't our first rodeo, but every time felt like stepping into the unknown.

"Listen up," I started, my voice steady, commanding attention. "We've got a situation that's going to need all our skills and then some. At 0600 hours, our Black Hawk went down in enemy territory. We have had no communication with the crew since the crash. As of now, their status is unknown, but we have to assume they're alive and waiting for extraction."

I paused, letting the gravity of the situation sink in. "Our mission is clear: locate our brothers, assess their condition, and extract them to safety. We don't leave anyone behind."

There was a smattering of 'Oorah, Sargent!' from the team.

Moving to the map laid out on the table, I pointed to the crash site marked in red. "This is where they went down. The area is hot, swarming with hostiles. We'll be inserting two clicks northwest of the site. Stealth is crucial. We go in under the cover of darkness, maintain radio silence, and use the terrain to our advantage."

I looked around the room, making eye contact with each team member. "Jones, you're on point for navigation. Keep us on track and out of sight. Martinez, you've got comms and tech. Make sure we stay in the loop with command and can get a signal out if we need to. Rodriguez, you're our medic. Prepare for the worst and hope for the best."

The room was filled with a tense energy as I continued. "We don't know what we're walking into. The enemy is unpredictable, and the terrain is unforgiving. But we've trained for this. We adapt, we overcome, and we complete our mission."

I could see the determination in their faces, the unspoken camaraderie that bound us together. "Pack your kits, double-check your gear, and be ready to move out in one hour. We're going to bring our guys home."

As the team dispersed to prepare, I took a moment to collect my thoughts. The mission was dangerous, the stakes high. But beyond the immediate danger lay the constant reminder of my promise to Emily. Her face flashed in my mind, her smile, the way her eyes lit up when she laughed. It was for her, for our future, that I had to get this mission done and come back home.

The team was ready, gear packed, faces set in grim determination. We moved to the transport, the hum of the engines a familiar comfort amidst the chaos of thoughts swirling in my mind. As the plane lifted off, taking us closer to the danger, to the unknown, I couldn't shake the image of Emily's face, a beacon of hope in the darkest of times.

"Duty and love," I whispered to myself, a silent vow that I would return to her, no matter what.

Unforeseen Colors

Emily

The large windows of my studio cast a gentle glow on the chaos of canvases and paint tubes strewn around. In this sacred space, amidst the scent of oil paint and turpentine, I found my peace, my purpose. Art was not just my passion; it was my sanctuary, a reflection of my innermost thoughts and emotions, a world where I could express myself unbound by the constraints of reality.

Each brushstroke was a whisper of my soul, a dance of light and shadow on the blank canvas, a palette of colors that told stories only the heart could understand. This upcoming show at the gallery wasn't just an exhibition; it was my opportunity, a chance to share my vision with the world, to make a mark that could redefine my future.

The gallery, with its elegant arches and soft, inviting lights, was more than just a building. It was a dream, a vision of what could be. I had spent countless hours walking through its halls, imagining my artwork adorning its walls, the vibrant colors of my paintings bringing life to its serene white space. Purchasing this gallery had become more than a wish—it was a goal, a tangible milestone that represented the culmination of my efforts, my dedication to my craft.

As I prepared for the upcoming art show, a torrent of emotions surged through me. I allowed my thoughts to drift beyond the immediate tasks at hand, beyond the canvases and paintbrushes, into the realm of what could be. The gallery, with its warm, inviting light and walls that whispered stories of countless artists before me, seemed to call out, echoing my deepest aspirations.

I imagined the gallery on the night of the show, alive with the hum of art enthusiasts and critics alike, all gathered in this sacred space of creativity to witness my work. The very thought sent waves of excitement mixed with a hint of nervousness through me. Each painting I planned to display was more than just color on canvas; they were fragments of my soul, meticulously crafted expressions of my deepest emotions and thoughts. To have them hung in such a revered venue, to share them with the world, was both a dream and a formidable challenge.

The gallery, nestled in the heart of our bustling town, had always been more than just a building to me. It was a haven of creativity, a central hub where artists and art lovers converged, where the vibrant pulse of the community could be felt most profoundly. And as I envisioned the space filled with people, their eyes alight with curiosity and appreciation, a deeper longing within me surfaced.

For as long as I could remember, I had harbored a secret dream – a dream of one day owning this very gallery. It wasn't a desire born out of vanity or a wish for control, but from a genuine love for the place and what it represented. I dreamt of turning it into an even more inclusive sanctuary, a place where artists, young and old, experienced and novices, could come together to learn, create, and share.

In my mind's eye, the gallery transformed under my stewardship. I saw walls adorned not only with traditional paintings but with dynamic interactive displays and digital art, reflecting the evolving nature of creativity. I envisioned lively workshops and open mic nights, where the community could gather to share stories and ideas, blurring the lines between artists and audience.

But more than just a place for art, I saw it as a beacon of inspiration and hope. I wanted to create programs for the youth, to nurture their creative sparks just as my own had been, to offer them a sanctuary from the pressures of the outside world and a chance to express themselves freely. I saw the gallery as a bridge, connecting the past with the future, the traditional with the avant-garde, the community with the individual.

This show, I realized, was more than just an opportunity to showcase my work; it was a step towards that larger dream. It was a chance to make a mark, to embed myself within the fabric of this artistic sanctuary, to lay the groundwork for a future where I could contribute even more profoundly to the community that had given me so much.

As I returned to my preparations, my heart swelled with a renewed sense of purpose. Yes, I was eager for recognition, for the chance to make a name for myself in the art world. But beyond the accolades and the fleeting spotlight, I yearned for something more enduring – the opportunity to make a lasting impact, to paint my own stroke in the vibrant mural of our town's cultural legacy. The gallery wasn't just a venue for my art; it was a symbol of what I hoped to achieve, a dream of fostering a space where creativity could flourish unbounded, enriching the lives of all who stepped through its welcoming doors.

But amidst the anticipation and the joy of creation, a shadow lingered, a reminder of the complexities of life beyond the canvas. Shane, with his easy smile and understanding eyes, was my unexpected muse, his presence igniting a flame of inspiration within me.

With each day, as the show drew nearer, I poured my heart into my paintings, channeling my emotions into every brushstroke, transforming my fears and dreams into vibrant landscapes of color and light. The gallery now felt within reach, a beacon of hope in the midst of uncertainty.

But amidst the chaos of creativity, a subtle but insistent sense of dissonance had crept in, a whisper in the back of my mind that something was amiss. I brushed it aside, attributing it to the nerves and the endless nights of painting, the coffee cups littering my studio proof of my relentless drive. Yet, as I added another brushstroke to the canvas, a realization dawned on me with chilling clarity—I had missed my cycle.

Panic clawed at my insides, a cold sweat breaking out as I put down the brush, the vibrant hues on the canvas mocking my sudden fear. How had I not noticed? The days had melded into one another, the hours consumed by my art, by the desperate need to keep my mind occupied, away from the void Shane's absence had left.

I couldn't be... could I? The thought was a tremor, shaking the foundations of the carefully constructed world I had built around me. Shane and I, our brief, intense connection had been a whirlwind, a passionate interlude in the otherwise structured canvas of my life. But with him gone, deployed to corners of the world where danger was a constant shadow, the idea of a life tethered to his, in such a permanent, undeniable way, was terrifying.

***

The pregnancy test now sitting ominously on my bathroom counter was a stark reminder of the my life with Shane, that continued despite his absence. I had been so caught up in my painting, in the chaotic whirlwind of colors and emotions, that I hadn't noticed the missed cycles, the subtle signs my body had been sending me. But there it was, undeniable proof of the life growing inside me—Shane's life, our life.

Shadows and light clashed on the canvas of my emotions as I envisioned the delicate pulse, a faint heartbeat painting its existence within me, echoing in the absence of its creator's touch.

The thought of Shane, out there in the unknown, weighed heavily on my mind. He was somewhere across the world, his life hanging in the balance every day, fighting in shadows while I stood here, surrounded by the safety and comfort of my studio. The dichotomy of our worlds, his fraught with danger and mine painted in serene strokes of blues and greens, seemed unfathomable, an unbridgeable gap between our current realities.

I needed to let him know about the baby, our baby. But how? He was on a mission shrouded in secrecy, a mission from which he might never return. The military's tight-lipped nature, the absence of contact, left me feeling helpless and isolated. The thought that he was out there, unaware of the life we had created, was unbearable. He deserved to know, to carry a piece of home with him, a flicker of hope on the relentless dark canvas of his duty.

I needed time, space to think and feel and decide. But the luxury of indecision was one I could ill afford. The truth, stark and undeniable, was a seed planted firmly in the reality of my being. I was pregnant, carrying a part of Shane, a tender, fragile link to the man who had stormed into my life and left a permanent brush stroke on my heart.

As I faced my reflection in the mirror, the truth stared back at me, a silent confirmation of the new life I was about to embark on. Fear, hope, and an overwhelming sense of protectiveness welled within me. This child, Shane's and mine, was evidence of a love that had defied the odds, a spark of something beautiful amidst the chaos of life.

Night after night, I wrestled with my choices, the studio my only witness. My art, once a source of solace, now reflected the turmoil within—a swirl of dark hues and jagged lines. The upcoming gallery show, a dream I had nurtured for so long, seemed insignificant against the backdrop of my personal storm.

In the quiet of the night, I would touch my still-flat belly, a silent conversation between me and the life that was growing inside. The world saw an artist, a woman coming into her own. But beneath the surface, I was a canvas unstretched, suspended between the ghostly afterimage of a vanished passion and the stark frame of reality.

As the show approached, the world around me seemed to slow, each moment heavy with significance. My studio, once a crucible of chaos and creation, had transformed into a sanctuary of reflection and revelation. The canvases that lined its walls were no longer just paintings; they were fragments of my soul, each one a chapter in the unwritten story of my life.

In the midst of this contemplative atmosphere, Mrs. Abbott, the gallery owner, visited my studio. Her presence brought a wave of reality into my secluded world, bridging the gap between my solitary creation process and the public exhibition awaiting. She walked among the canvases with a reverence that matched my own, her eyes reflecting the depth and emotion I had poured into each piece.

"Emily," Mrs. Abbott began, her voice breaking the silence, "your work has always captivated me, but this collection—it's exceptional. There's a truth in these paintings, a raw honesty that's rare."

I felt a blush of pride but also a surge of gratitude. Mrs. Abbott had offered me more than wall space in her gallery; she had provided a platform for my voice, my vision. "Thank you," I replied, "Your gallery has become a part of me, of my artistic journey. It's not just a space; it's a sanctuary for artists like me, a place where we can share our inner worlds without fear."

She smiled, understanding the weight of my words. "You know, Emily, I've always seen more than just talent in you. I've seen a kindred spirit, someone who understands the soul of my gallery. It's more than a business to me; it's a legacy, a piece of the town's heart."

The conversation shifted subtly, and a thread of hope wove its way through my thoughts. "Mrs. Abbott," I hesitated, gathering my courage, "I've dreamt of one day taking on a role like yours, nurturing this community's culture and spirit through art. I've imagined myself continuing the legacy you've built, shaping the gallery into an even more inclusive beacon of creativity."

Her eyes, wise and warm, met mine. "I've always known the gallery would need someone passionate to carry on its legacy, someone who loves this place as much as I do. Emily, I've seen how the townspeople and tourists alike are drawn here, not just to the art, but to the ambiance, the sense of belonging. You understand that magic; you're part of its very fabric."

The idea of owning the gallery, of being the custodian of such an essential piece of our town's cultural heritage, had always been a distant dream. But as Mrs. Abbott spoke, the dream flickered to life, tangible and within reach.

"Our town needs its artists, its visionaries," Mrs. Abbott continued, "and it needs places like the gallery to remind us all of the beauty that life holds, of the new perspectives waiting to be seen. Emily, I believe you could be the one to carry this torch forward, to paint your own colors onto the legacy of this place."

Her words settled over me like a mantle, heavy with possibility and responsibility. The gallery, with its warm lights and welcoming doors, had always been more to me than a building; it was a symbol of community, of art transcending the confines of individual experience to speak universal truths.

As Mrs. Abbott left, her words lingered, painting new visions of the future in my mind. The gallery could become an extension of my own passion for art, a place where the community could gather not just to observe, but to participate, to paint their own colors onto the ongoing mural of our cultural heritage.

***

In the quiet of my studio, surrounded by the silent witnesses of my artistic journey, I allowed myself to dream bigger than I had ever dared before. The upcoming show was no longer just an exhibition; it was the beginning of a new chapter, an invitation to step into a larger role within the heartbeat of our town.

In the stillness of my sanctuary, I found myself standing before the largest canvas, its surface a tumult of colors and emotions, mirroring the storm within me. My hand hovered, brush poised, as if waiting for a sign. And then, in the quiet, I felt it—a gentle flutter, like the softest brushstroke against the canvas of my belly. It was a reminder, a whisper from the life growing inside me, intertwining with the essence of Shane, binding us together across the vastness of absence and uncertainty.

This tiny flutter was a revelation, a brushstroke of hope on the vast canvas of my future. It was as if the baby was painting its own presence, coloring my world with new shades of love and fear, of hope and uncertainty. In that moment, I understood that no matter what lay ahead, this child, our child, would be my greatest masterpiece, a living testament to the love Shane and I shared, to the enduring power of art to heal and reveal, to confront and comfort.

With renewed purpose, I approached my art, my perspective shifted. The paintings for the show took on new life, each one a step towards understanding, a move towards acceptance. I painted with the knowledge that every stroke was a legacy, a message to the future, a piece of myself that would live on, telling our story, Shane's and mine, and now, this new life's.

The gallery show was no longer just an exhibition; it was a declaration, a celebration of life in all its complexity. I realized then that the gallery I so longed to make my own was more than a space for art—it was a home for the stories we tell, for the emotions we share, and for the connections that bind us, even in absence.

As I placed the final touch on the last piece, stepping back to see the culmination of my work, I felt a peace settle over me. I was ready. Ready to face the world, to share my vision, to embrace the unknown. The gallery awaited, not just as a showcase for my art, but as a witness to my journey, a bridge between my past and my future.

In the silence of the night, I placed my hand on my belly, speaking silently to Shane, to our unborn child, promising them both that no matter what the future held, we would face it together, through the legacy of love and art we had created. In that moment, I was no longer adrift between past and present, but anchored in the certainty of my own strength, in the unwavering light of hope that guides us through the darkest of times.

***

I stood before the threshold of the gallery, a portal between my past and the vast, uncharted future. Today, the gallery transformed from a mere building to a vessel of my dreams, each piece of art a heartbeat, a breath, a step on the journey of self-discovery and resilience.

With every brushstroke laid bare for the world to see, I realized that this exhibition was not just a display of art; it was a narrative of survival, of the undying human spirit that thrives in the face of adversity. The paintings, vibrant with the story of our shared past, Shane's and mine, and the silent whisper of the life we created, spoke of a love that transcended the confines of time and circumstance.

I entered the gallery, the air filled with anticipation, the walls echoing the silent conversations between artist and observer. Each canvas was an open letter, a shared secret, a bridge connecting my inner world with those who dared to step inside. The colors, textures, and shapes, once confined to the privacy of my studio, now stood as witness to the journey of a woman who faced the tempest of uncertainty and emerged with a new vision, a new purpose.

As guests began to fill the gallery, the atmosphere turned electric with anticipation and admiration. Their eyes, wide with curiosity, darted from one painting to another, each canvas telling a story, each brushstroke a secret whispered in color. The gallery, once a beacon of my dreams, had transformed into a vibrant stage for my innermost expressions.

A group of enthusiasts, their gazes fixed on a particularly vivid portrayal of the seaside, beckoned me over. Their eagerness was palpable, their smiles wide with genuine interest. "Emily," one of them started, her voice laced with intrigue, "this piece is breathtaking. Can you tell us what inspired it?"

The question, so direct and full of admiration, sparked a warmth within me. Standing before my own creations, sharing their origins, I felt an unprecedented sense of pride and connection. "This piece," I began, my voice steady yet filled with emotion, "is inspired by childhood memories, of days spent by the sea, where the vastness of the ocean met the endless possibilities of the sky."

The group listened intently, their eyes reflecting the scenes I described, as if witnessing the memories themselves. The conversation flowed seamlessly, from the inspiration behind each painting to the techniques I employed to capture the fleeting moments of beauty and turmoil alike. The thrill of discussing my work, of seeing others moved by my artistic narrative, was exhilarating, a validation of my silent conversations with the canvas.

As the evening unfolded, more guests approached, each conversation a thread adding to the rich tapestry of the night. Compliments were offered, questions posed, and, to my growing delight, inquiries about purchasing my paintings began to emerge. Each sale felt like a triumph, not just for my bank account, but for my soul. It was as if every piece sold carried a part of me with it, a fragment of my story painted into the lives of others.

The excitement in the gallery was palpable, the air charged with the energy of discovery and recognition. I moved among the guests, a part of me still in disbelief that this was my life, that these were my paintings eliciting such profound reactions. The success of the evening was more than just the sales, though they were a welcome bonus. It was the acknowledgment of my art, the realization that what I created resonated deeply with others.

Amid the hum of conversation and the clinking of glasses, I found a moment of quiet reflection. The gallery, with its soft lighting and walls adorned with my emotions, felt like a sanctuary. Here, in this sacred space, art and life converged, telling stories of love, loss, and hope. The echoes of my past love, the vivid reality of my present, and the promise of a new life all merged into a symphony of colors, a testament to the journey I had undertaken.

Tonight, the gallery was not just a setting for my art; it was a testament to my journey, from the shadows of doubt to the light of acceptance and recognition. As I mingled with the guests, their words of praise and contemplation echoing in my ears, I realized that this was more than an exhibition; it was a celebration of life's unfathomable beauty, of the resilience of the human spirit, and of the unbreakable bond between artist and observer. In this space, we were all part of something greater, a shared experience transcending the ordinary, captured in the timeless dance of color and light on canvas.

In this moment, surrounded by the tangible results of my passion and pain, I realized that art was my truest voice, my most faithful companion through the journey of life. It was through this medium that I could express the inexpressible, share the unshareable, and connect with others in a profound and meaningful way.

As I stood there, my hand resting gently on the barely discernable curve of my belly, I whispered a silent vow to the life within me and to Shane, who would be here if he could. "This is for us," I said, a promise that no matter where the tides of life may take us, our story would continue, through the legacy we leave behind, through the lives we touch with our love and our art.

Today, I was more than an artist; I was a storyteller, a keeper of memories, a beacon of hope. I was a mother-to-be, carrying the future, nurturing a new life forged from love and shaped by the trials of life. I knew that this exhibition was not the end but a beautiful beginning, the first stroke on the blank canvas of our future.

Echoes Through the Jungle: A Promise Unyielded

Shane

The jungle teems around me, dense leaves and tangled vines resisting every step. Moving feels like wading through thick water, each motion slow, deliberate. The heavy air suffocates, worse than any humid summer night in Macon, turning breaths into labor. Anxiety is my constant companion, buzzing incessantly in my head. Deep in enemy lands, shadows morph into potential threats, every rustle of leaves could herald an ambush. Our mission weighs heavily on me: we're here to retrieve our fallen comrades, their memory a somber echo in each heartbeat.

As we trudge forward, the past plays tricks on me, blending with the sound of distant gunfire. I think back to when I first met Johnson, how his grin could cut through the darkest times, a sharp contrast to our current grim surroundings. Then there's Martinez, the guy who could outthink anyone, his silent strategies now just whispers among the leaves.

But it's not just them filling my thoughts. My mind drifts further back, to softer, warmer memories. I remember long, lazy days by the river with Emily, her laughter mingling with the water's flow, her touch light as a breeze. Her presence in my recollections feels so strong, it's as if she's right here, her hand brushing mine, pulling me back from the edge.

The smell of gramma's kitchen, the comfort of sunlight breaking through the trees back home – they all weave together with thoughts of Emily. Her smile, the way her eyes lit up when she laughed, it all comes flooding back, grounding me. These memories, they're more than just echoes of a simpler time; they are my beacon, guiding me through the chaos, reminding me what's waiting on the other side of this endless night. We march on, and with each step, it's her face I see, urging me forward, reminding me why we endure.

The damp earth beneath my boots releases a mix of scents — fresh mud, decaying leaves, and the distant, yet unmistakable, tang of salt from a nearby stream. The air changes as we move deeper, from oppressive heat to a sudden chill as clouds gather above, a whisper of rain threatening to break the heavy silence. Around us, the jungle is a constant cacophony: insects chirping, the distant call of an unknown bird, the rustle of leaves that might be the wind — or might not. Each sound, each smell is a reminder of where we are, far from the concrete and steel of home, submerged in nature's untamed heart.

I lead silently, each signal a command honed by training and trust. The dense undergrowth challenges every step, but we move as shadows, leaving no trace, our eyes constantly scanning for the unseen enemy. We're a unit, moving in sync, covering each other's backs, our movements almost silent against the backdrop of the jungle's natural sounds. The tension is a tangible thing, thick as the foliage we navigate, but our resolve is stronger, forged in the fires of shared trials and tribulations.

As we inch closer to the site, my gut twists tighter. We're deep in the belly of the beast, every shadow a potential enemy, every rustle a call to arms. I can't help but wonder, are we the hunters or the hunted? The crash site finally comes into view.

The wreckage is scattered, broken, bleakly telling the story, the violence of their fall. My eyes scan the clearing, heart sinking as they land on the fallen. In the clearing, amidst the discordant symphony of the jungle's life, the reality of war became tangible in the most harrowing way. As we secured the perimeter, my gaze shifted to our comrades, the land now a part of them, just as they had become a part of it. Two lay motionless, their expressions locked in an eerie tranquility that belied the chaos of their final moments. It was a surreal contrast that left an indelible mark on my heart.

But among the stillness, there were survivors, each one proof of the tenacity of the human spirit. Their battered forms were etched with the brutal narrative of survival, yet in their eyes, there shimmered a fragile glint of hope. As I knelt beside them, the air was thick with the unspoken bond of soldiers who had faced the abyss together.

One of the wounded, Corporal Cullen, caught my eye. His breaths were shallow, each one a struggle against the pain. With effort, he leaned closer, his voice a mere whisper, breaking the heavy silence. "The rotor... it clipped a tree on the way down," he gasped, the words punctuated by grimaces of pain. "It was chaos, man... chaos in the sky before everything went black."

I nodded, my hand instinctively finding his shoulder, a meager comfort in the vastness of his suffering. The details were sparse, but they painted a vivid picture of the sudden, disorienting descent — a routine patrol turned nightmare.

Another, Sergeant Buchanan, with bandages stark against her skin, turned her head with evident effort. "We were flying low, avoiding radar," she whispered, her voice tinged with the fatigue of one who has cheated death. "Then, just... noise, and spinning, and... then this." She gestured weakly to the wreckage, to the broken bodies, to the mangled metal now reclaimed by nature.

Each account, each whispered confession, added layers to the tragedy, sketching a stark mosaic of fate and fortitude. I moved among them, listening, affirming, sharing in the silent language of grief and camaraderie. These whispered conversations, though fleeting, were heavy with the weight of shared ordeal, binding us together in the solemn fraternity of the wounded and the lost.

In the clearing, surrounded by the evidence of our ordeal, the juxtaposition of life and death, of serenity and violence, I felt an overwhelming sense of responsibility. These men and women, my brothers and sisters in arms, had faced the unimaginable, and it was our duty to bear witness, to carry their stories and their sacrifices beyond the confines of this jungle tomb.

We spring into action, gathering both the living and the dead. Marines never leave a man behind. But as we tend to their wounds, I can't shake the feeling of eyes on us, the jungle seeming to pause, waiting for something. We're not just fighting time, but the unseen enemy, always lurking, always waiting. The weight of our mission, the lives in our hands, it's a heavy burden, but one we carry not just willingly, but proudly. For them. For each other.

We move cautiously, every sense heightened, aware that the enemy could be lurking behind any tree or underbrush, especially now that they must know about the crash. We communicate with hand signals, our voices a luxury we can't afford here. Our journey back is slow, weighted down by our injured comrades and the solemn burden of those we've lost.

The tension is like a tight wire in the air, every snapped twig or distant call making us pause, hearts racing. We're a chain of determination, each of us a link, supporting the wounded, carrying our fallen, never breaking. The path we choose is indirect, zigzagging, avoiding the obvious routes that could be watched. Every step is placed with care, every pause full of silent prayers that we remain unseen.

As we inch closer to safety, every muscle in my body screams for rest, but there's no room for weakness, not here, not now. The jungle, once merely an obstacle, now feels like an adversary, dense and unyielding, clawing at us with every step. Our breaths come in short, ragged gasps, a canvas of exhaustion under the oppressive heat.

The silence around us grows, an unnatural quiet that heightens our senses, a stark contrast to the constant hum of life we've grown accustomed to. It's as if even the creatures of this place sense the impending danger, retreating into their hidden burrows. My heart pounds, a relentless brush stroke in my chest, echoing the silent alarm that rings clear in this sudden void. We're close, so close to the extraction point, but this silence, this break in the jungle's eternal whisper, it's a harbinger.

I can feel the eyes on us, hidden watchers in the foliage, and I know we're walking into a trap, our every move watched, calculated. But we push forward, because hesitation is a luxury we can't afford, our resolve hardened by the promise of what lies just beyond the treeline. The jungle, once a mere oppressive backdrop, transforms abruptly into a living nightmare. Each leaf seems to quiver with malicious intent as we inch forward, the air thick with unspoken dread. The silence is suffocating, heavier than the humid air pressing against my skin. It's in this unbearable quiet that my heart screams for Emily, for the serene echo of our shared laughter by the Ocmulgee River, a stark contrast to the impending doom that I can feel tightening around us like a noose.

Without warning, the world erupts into chaos. Gunshots shatter the silence, each report slicing through the calm memories of summer days spent with her. I'm thrown into motion, my actions mechanical, honed by training yet fueled by raw, unbridled fear. The lush greenery, once a picturesque backdrop for whispered promises of love, morphs into a horrific artwork of shadow and fire. Bullets zip through the air, invisible harbingers of death, their paths marked only by the destruction they leave in their wake.

I'm shouting orders, the sounds torn from my throat, harsh and foreign. My squad, my responsibility, scatters, each man a flurry of desperate action amidst the bedlam. The foliage around us, so similar to the underbrush Emily and I had once lain in together, watching the stars, becomes a sinister maze, each branch a potential omen of doom.

As I dive for cover, the ground harsh against my skin, flashes of Emily pierce the terror. Her eyes, bright with unshed tears as we said our goodbyes, now stark against the carnage unfolding before me. The juxtaposition is jarring, her face a beacon of peace amidst the horror, grounding me even as the earth seems to tilt beneath me.

The battle rages, a mix of sounds — the sharp staccato of gunfire, the thud of bodies hitting the ground, the cries of the wounded. I move, firing back, each pull of the trigger a desperate plea for survival, for the chance to return to her arms. With every shot fired, I see her face, a painful reminder of what I'm fighting for, of the world beyond this hellish landscape.

An explosion rocks the ground near me, a deafening roar that echoes the turmoil in my heart. I'm thrown to the side, disoriented, the world a blur of motion and noise. In the haze of pain and confusion, Emily's face is my anchor, her voice a distant lullaby amidst the cacophony of war. The ground meets my back with a jarring thud, and for a moment, I'm floating, adrift between two worlds — one filled with the horrors of war, the other with the gentle caress of love.

Blood, warm and sticky, trickles into my eyes, a stark contrast to the gentle touch of her fingers brushing my cheek. The pain is grounding, a vicious reminder of the present, pulling me back from the precipice of surrender. I claw my way back to reality, her face a vision in my mind, a vow of return whispered with every labored breath.

I struggle to my feet, the world tilting dangerously, each movement proof of the human will to survive, to return to those they love. The battle rages around me, but within, a different war is waged — one of memory against reality, of love against despair.

The jungle's thick around me, closing in like the night does back home. But there's no comfort here, no familiar stars overhead, just the heavy darkness and the lingering stench of gunpowder and blood. Each step is harder than the last, like my boots are filled with lead, not just mud.

I keep pushing through, though. Got to. There's this image of a woman that won't leave me alone. Her laughing, her joking around, the way she'd look at me as if I was the only one in the world. That's what I'm walking towards, what I'm fighting to get back to. It's not about being a hero; it's about getting back to her, to that peace she represents.

The gunfire's died down now, or maybe my ears have just stopped working right. Doesn't matter. I'm too tired to care, too worn out to be scared anymore. I'm hurt, I know that much, but admitting it feels like giving up, and that's not an option. Not yet. Not until I'm out of this hell.

We're Marines; we don't leave anyone behind, dead or alive. Oorah! That's what keeps us going, that unspoken promise to each other. But in my head, there's another promise. One I made to who? The face in my memory, and it's echoing with every heartbeat.

Suddenly, the ground's coming up fast, and I realize I'm falling. No strength left to stop it. As I hit the dirt, it's like all the sounds of the jungle rush back at me, loud and clear. But over all that noise, there's a quiet voice inside me whispering a name I can't quite remember.

Lying there, face in the mud, I think of her. Not the way she was when I left, all tears and tight smiles, but the way she'd be on a normal day, sunshine in her hair, eyes full of life. That's the memory I hold onto, the one that's got to last me, because I'm not sure I'm getting out of this.

But I can't let it end here, not like this, not without seeing her again. So I push myself up, using what's left of my strength, driven by that single thought. I don't know if I'm crawling or walking or dragging myself along, but I'm moving, damn it. Because of her. For her. But who is she!

The darkness edges in, and I know I'm close, close to passing out or maybe something worse. But there's a part of me that's okay with it, knowing I kept fighting, kept trying to get back. If I have to go out, at least I'm going out thinking of her, carrying that bit of peace with me.

Then everything fades, and the last thing I cling to is the hope that somehow, she knows I didn't give up. That I tried, for her.

And then, it's just black.

Colors of Resilience: Embracing the Unknown

Emily

The space around me stretches, vast and expectant, as I face the towering blankness of the canvas. It stands before me, not just as a piece of fabric but as a battleground, where I come, not as an artist, but as a warrior armed with brush and palette, ready to confront my own tempest.

With a force that surprises even me, I drag the brush across the canvas, letting out a silent cry as a stream of crimson invades the white. It's more than just paint—it's my pain, my desperation, spilling over, unable to be contained any longer. I plunge the brush into ultramarine, feeling the weight of its depth, and hurl it against the canvas, watching as my turmoil splatters, blending with my fears, my anger, my unanswered questions about Shane.

My breathing turns heavy, labored, each exhale a brushstroke, each inhale a preparation for the next assault. I circle the easel like it's the center of my storm, moving to a rhythm pounded out by my own heart, my steps barely disturbing the newspapers beneath my feet, a testament to days and nights spent here, seeking, pleading, aching.

The studio, my haven of peace, now resonates with the echoes of my struggle. Tubes of paint, my comrades in arms, lie scattered and open, their colors melding on the workbench in an unpremeditated alliance. The air is heavy with the scent of oil and turpentine, thick with the residue of my endless battles against the silence, against the absence.

A harsh stroke sends a jar of brushes clattering to the floor. The sound crashes through the silence, a discordant stroke in the symphony of my chaos, disrupting the rhythm of my brushstrokes as if splattering unwelcome droplets on a meticulously crafted watercolor. I stop, breath caught, caught up in the raw, vivid testament to my inner world sprawling before me. For a moment, the relentless tide of waiting, of wondering, of the heavy cloak of the unknown, falls away, and it's just me, my canvas, and the raw, naked truth of my fears and hopes.

I reach for a shade of light azure, the color of the skies I'm yearning to see clear again. With a touch softened by memory, I guide the brush across the turmoil, weaving calm into the heart of the storm. This act, gentler than the ones before, soothes not just the canvas but something deep within me. Amid the fury, I find a whisper of strength, a reminder that within the chaos of my heart lies not just a storm, but an endless, serene sky.

Each stroke on the canvas carries a silent prayer for Shane, a word left hanging in our shared space, a dream clinging stubbornly to hope.

My hand pauses, resting gently on my slightly rounded belly, a constant reminder of the life we've created together. The pregnancy, a joyous revelation weeks ago, now serves as a stark reminder of Shane's absence. The fear of raising our child alone creeps in like an unwanted shadow, darkening the edges of my thoughts. I turn back to my canvas, my refuge, letting the colors speak the words I cannot find, painting my hopes and fears into the silent, waiting surface.

In the weeks that follow, each day in my studio becomes a journey through an emotional landscape, marked by the rhythm of my heartbeat and the stroke of my brush. I watch as the canvas morphs, reflecting the tumultuous sea of my thoughts. Dark, swirling blues and oppressive greys dominate early pieces, their chaotic swirls a mirror to the storm within me. I mix the paints, watching as they bleed into each other like the blending of fear with hope, the sharp contrast echoing the uncertainty of Shane's fate.

I work tirelessly, the studio my sanctuary from the relentless march of time, each painting a chapter in a story only I know the full depth of. I find myself talking to Shane through my art, asking silent questions to which I receive no answers. The colors become more intense, more vivid, a riot on the senses as my feelings pour out, unfiltered and raw.

Bright flashes of red and orange start to break through the darkness, representing bursts of anger and frustration, a fiery testament to the strength of my love and the pain of separation. I layer the paint thickly, creating textures that beg to be touched, to be understood just as I long to understand why this is happening to us. The brush trembles slightly in my grasp, not from the draft that occasionally sweeps through the studio, which I've learned to ignore, but from the tumult of emotions roiling within me. As I blend a new hue, striving to capture a fleeting memory, the abrupt ring of the phone shatters my cocoon of concentration, a stark discord in the harmony of my solitude.

I pause, brush halted mid-stroke, heart thundering against my ribcage. Silence has been my constant companion for days, and suddenly, I'm paralyzed between longing for a connection and the dread of unwelcome news. Each ring slices through the stillness, a reminder of the world beyond my canvas, laden with possibilities and fears.

On the third ring, I muster the remnants of my resolve and pick up, my voice a mere echo of itself, "Hello?"

"Em, it's Lily," comes the response, wrapped in warmth yet tinged with an undercurrent of concern. "First, I love you. I've been thinking about you...a lot. And I've got something for you. Can I come over?"

A wave of relief momentarily washes over me, quickly shadowed by a faint twinge of disappointment — still no word from Shane. But Lily's thoughtfulness, the familiar comfort of family, slowly thaws the edges of my self-imposed isolation. "Yes, come over," I reply, finding a shred of comfort in the prospect. "I'd appreciate that. I love you, more."

Soon, a gentle tap on the door announces her arrival. Lily steps into the chaos of my sanctuary, arms filled with bags that chime softly, heralding new paints, brushes, perhaps a piece of the outside world she's bringing into mine. Her eyes roam the clutter of canvases and colors, a silent indication of my inner storm, yet they hold no judgment, only understanding.

"These are for you," she says, her voice a balm, as she sets down the supplies. "I saw these and... I just knew they were meant for you, for your journey." Her smile wavers but doesn't falter, a bridge across the chasm of unspoken words between us.

Her kindness, the empathy behind the gesture, reaches through the fog of my solitude, offering a glimmer of light. Together, we unpack the supplies, and I share with her my most recent creation — a tumultuous blend of despair and hope captured in oil and canvas. Lily observes in silence, then whispers, "It's hauntingly beautiful, Em. He would be so proud."

Her attempt to comfort slices through me, a reminder of the gaping absence I navigate each day. Turning from the canvas, I fight the surge of emotions her words unleash. "I can't feel him anymore, Lily. It's like with each passing day, he's just... fading away."

She steps closer, her presence a solid, comforting reality, her hand resting gently on my arm. "But he's here, Em, in every piece you create. You're weaving him into your life, into your art, in the most beautiful way. You're not alone in this. And you also have your nugget." Lily's affectionate term for our baby.

Lily's simple, heartfelt words chip away at the walls I've built around my grief. My sister has always been a source of strength for me. For the first time in what feels like an eternity, I lean into the comfort offered, allowing the shared silence that follows to envelop me, filled with an unspoken understanding that transcends words.

Together, we face the canvas once again, and I pick up the brush, my movements steadier for the presence of my sister. Lily doesn't need to speak as I return to my painting; her steadfast support fortifies me, a quiet reminder that in the midst of my turmoil, I am anchored by love and family. In the silent companionship, my fears recede, if only for a moment.

The shift from fear to using art as a coping mechanism was gradual, unfolding with each day spent in my studio. Initially, my hands trembled with each stroke, the colors on the palette mirroring the chaos within me. Dark, ominous shades dominated, the physical act of painting becoming a release for the pent-up terror and despair. But as days passed, painting became more than just an outlet for fear; it transformed into a ritual, a time for reflection and solace.

I began to experiment with lighter shades, allowing soft pastels to infiltrate the canvas, intermingling with the stormy blues and grays. This mingling of colors mirrored my internal battle, the struggle between despair and burgeoning hope. The act of blending, of creating something new from the rawness of my emotions, offered a strange comfort. My brushstrokes became more deliberate, each one a step toward acceptance, a testament to resilience. These colors speaking of the strength I didn't know I had, the resolve to face whatever future comes, for me, for our child, for Shane.

As I smear a deep, cerulean blue across the sky of my canvas, my mind drifts, unbidden, to a day last summer when Shane and I had watched the sun dip below the horizon, painting the world in a similar hue. He had turned to me, eyes reflecting the twilight, and whispered, "You know, Em, this is the color of dreams."

A soft chuckle escapes my lips, the memory so vivid it's as if he's right beside me. "And what do you dream of, Shane?" I had asked, leaning into his warmth.

His hand had found mine, fingers intertwining. "A future," he'd said, "with you, in a place where every day ends like this." His voice echoes in my studio, a tender ghost woven through the streaks of my brush.

Tears prick at the corners of my eyes, blurring the line between past and present. "I'm trying to hold onto that dream, Shane," I whisper into the empty room, the ache in my chest widening. "But it's hard without you here."

The silence that follows feels oppressive, a stark reminder of his absence. Shaking off the sorrow, I force myself to focus on the canvas, my hand moving with renewed purpose. "You told me to paint our dreams," I murmur, as if he can hear me. "So that's what I'll do."

A new layer of paint, lighter now, begins to transform the scene. I imagine Shane standing behind me, his chin resting on my shoulder. "You're bringing the light back," I hear his voice in my mind, encouraging, warm.

"I'm trying," I admit, allowing the fantasy to soothe the raw edges of my reality. "But I wish you were here to see it. To tell me it's going to be okay."

The imagined weight of his hands on my shoulders steadies me, a comforting pressure that's both memory and wishful thinking. "It's going to be beautiful, Em," he says in my head, his optimism as infectious now as it had always been.

With each brushstroke, the dialogue continues, a blend of memory and longing, shaping the painting into something more than just colors and forms. It becomes a dialogue between what was and what I desperately hope can be again. In this quiet studio, surrounded by the whispers of our past and the strokes of a future I'm still painting, I find a fragile peace, a momentary reprieve in the canvas of our shared dreams.

The physicality of painting – the smell of the oils, the feel of the brush in my hand, the sight of emerging beauty from the gloom – became a grounding ritual. In the sanctuary of my studio, amid the swirl of colors, I found a semblance of peace, a space where I could hold onto Shane's memory and face the uncertainty of our future with a newfound strength.

As I continue to paint, the evolution in my artwork becomes unmistakable. Initially dominated by a palette of stormy grays and somber blues, my canvases gradually welcome the warmth of sunnier shades. I find solace in the physical act of mixing paints, the way bright oranges and soft pinks blend on the palette, reminiscent of the sky at dawn.

These new colors bring a different energy, infusing my pieces with a sense of hope and renewal. With each brushstroke, I weave my fears, my love, and my unwavering hope into a visual diary. The transformation is cathartic; through the medium of paint, I confront my reality and mold it into something new, something hopeful. The vibrancy on the canvas is a stark contrast to the initial despair, symbolizing not just the dawn of a new day but the strength found in facing my deepest fears head-on.

As I stand back, the emotions wash over me, each canvas a chapter of my inner journey. One painting, with its tumultuous waves of dark blue and black, vividly encapsulates my deepest fears, the turmoil Shane's silence brought. Another, where light breaks through a stormy sky, symbolizes hope—a reflection of my stubborn belief in brighter days. This evolution in my work, from despair to cautious optimism, mirrors my own growth.

A soft knock interrupts my contemplation. I clean my hands and approach the door, revealing Jenna, her eyes alight with the kind of fervor only true friends can harbor.

"Emily, these are magnificent," she declares, her gaze sweeping over the pieces that chronicle my pain, my love, my silent cries for Shane. "It's time, Em. Everyone needs to see this."

Hesitation grips me, the familiar weight of uncertainty. "But Jenna, are we ready? Is this the right time?" The thought of exposing my raw emotions to the world makes my heart skip.

She steps forward, her presence a grounding force. "This is exactly the right time. Remember, this was the plan — your beautiful work in The Art Gallery. She believes in you, we all do. And Grandma is so excited to host your debut."

The reminder steadies me. Mrs. Abbott, Jenna's grandmother, had been more than a mentor; she was a believer in the healing power of art, seeing in my paintings a story that transcended personal grief and spoke to universal experiences.

"You're right," I find myself saying, the words forming a bridge over my doubts. "I've been painting for this moment, haven't I?"

Jenna's smile is all the answer I need. "Let's start planning. Grandma has been preparing the gallery, envisioning where each piece should go. She's as invested in this as we are."

After Jenna leaves, the studio seems transformed, no longer a place of confinement but a launching pad for a broader journey. I turn to the painting that started it all, the embodiment of my darkest and brightest moments. It's more than canvas and paint; it's a piece of my heart, soon to be exposed under Mrs. Abbott's careful stewardship.

Emboldened, I begin preparing my final piece for the show, infused with the realization that this exhibition is a culmination of more than just my efforts; it's the shared vision of those who have stood by me — Jenna, Mrs. Abbott, my family and even Shane, in spirit.

***

The excitement leading up to the gallery showing is palpable. I spend days, then hours, fussing over the placement of each piece, ensuring the lighting casts the perfect glow on my canvases. Invitations sent out weeks ago have garnered enthusiastic responses, and now, the community's buzz has reached a fever pitch. My heart races with anticipation and a touch of nervousness. This is more than a showing; it's a revelation of my innermost journey, a raw, public unveiling of my soul. Amidst the flurry of preparations, I can't help but feel a blend of exhilaration and fear, wondering how my story, painted in bold strokes and vivid colors, will be received. But beneath it all lies a deeper yearning, a silent hope that somehow, Shane will know, will feel the love and longing I've poured into each piece.

As friends, family, and community members wander through the gallery, the atmosphere is electric with anticipation and emotion. I notice the wide-eyed admiration of a long-time neighbor, her gaze moving from piece to piece, pausing to absorb every detail. A close friend, who has watched my journey from the sidelines, approaches me with tears in her eyes, whispering, "I had no idea..." Her words trail off, but her hug says everything.

My parents, always supportive but often worried, share looks of quiet pride and relief as they overhear the glowing comments and see the genuine reactions of the crowd. Conversations around me bubble with excitement, with phrases like "incredible depth" and "raw emotion" floating to my ears, grounding me in the reality that my work, my story, is resonating.

Elaine and Lily, my sisters, weave through the crowd, their faces alight with a mix of pride and surprise. Elaine, ever the stoic, has tears glistening in her eyes as she pulls me into a tight embrace, murmuring, "This is incredible, Em. Truly." Lily, with her infectious enthusiasm, bounces from painting to painting, exclaiming to anyone who'll listen, "Can you believe she's my sister?" Their genuine reactions, a blend of familial pride and awe, bolster my spirits, intertwining their joy with the collective energy of the night.

Amidst the praise, I find a moment of solace, feeling Shane's absence but also his presence in the shared space of art and understanding. The looks on the faces around me—some of joy, others of poignant understanding—bring a bittersweet sense of accomplishment. I realize then that this night, this exhibition, is a turning point, not just in my career, but in my personal journey through fear and love towards a hopeful future.

As the night progresses I realize I've sold enough pieces to not just dream about owning the gallery, but actually do it. As we celebrate, the gallery owner approaches with an offer that's within reach, thanks to the night's success. The realization that I can actually own the gallery sweeps over me like a wave. It's an electrifying moment; my dream, once sketched out in hesitant thoughts and uncertain wishes, is now within my grasp.

The energy in the room is infectious, and I can't help but get caught up in it. The pride in my family's eyes, the congratulations from friends and patrons, it all adds layers to the reality setting in. This success, borne from my deepest fears and hopes, cements my resolve to build a future, one brushstroke at a time, with or without Shane. The future, once clouded and uncertain, now stretches before me, a canvas waiting for new dreams, new colors. Amidst the joy and disbelief, Shane's absence is a shadow on my heart. Every sale, every word of praise, I wish he could share in this moment. My dream of owning the gallery is becoming real, but it's bittersweet without him to celebrate with me. My love for him, entwined with my success tonight, fuels a silent promise to keep our shared dreams alive until he can stand beside me again.

Echoes of the Forgotten

Shane

Waking up in a strange place, the dim light seeping through the thatched roof of a small hut, I'm totally confused. The air carries unfamiliar scents, a mixture of earth and woodsmoke, while outside, the distant sounds of village life – children's laughter, the rhythmic thud of pestle against mortar – create a backdrop to my disoriented thoughts. My body aches, wrapped in bandages not my own, lying on a bed made of materials I can't recognize. The villagers, kind faces etched with concern, speak in a tongue that dances around my comprehension, their words somehow familiar yet alien.

Frustration gnaws at me as I try to communicate, grasping for words that feel just out of reach. I am a stranger here, not only to these people but to myself. The only anchor in the swirl of lost memories is the fleeting image of a woman – her smile, the light in her eyes – a brushstroke of bright color against the gray canvas of my amnesia. Her face haunts my waking moments and my dreams, a puzzle piece disconnected from the rest.

Even though the people in the village are trying to help me get better, I still can't remember anything. The more they try to help, the more lost I feel, trapped between a world that's caring for me and a past that's just shadows and whispers. I try desperately to remember who I am, but I can't find any answers. I feel stuck and alone, even though the people around me are kind and try to help. It's like I'm fighting with myself, wanting so badly to remember my old life, but everything is just too foggy.

***

Physically, I'm healed, but there's an emptiness, a lack of direction that keeps me anchored here among the villagers. Without memories to guide me, I have no past to return to, no future to move towards. The villagers have become my temporary family, my shelter in this storm of confusion, but this isn't my home. Every morning I wake up under a foreign roof, I'm reminded of my lost self, stranded in a place that's kind but not mine. The frustration gnaws at me; I'm healed on the outside but aimless, like a blank canvas, waiting for that first brushstroke. The villagers welcome my help with open arms, teaching me their ways in return. "Tuoma," they call me, a reminder of my lost past every time it's spoken. I join them in the fields, learning the rhythm of their work, sharing smiles even when words fail us. "Good, Tuoma," one laughs, as I clumsily handle a farming tool. Nights are filled with shared meals and stories told in halting language. In these moments, I find a semblance of belonging, yet the gap in my memory casts a long shadow, keeping me tethered to a past I can't reach.

Each morning, as the village comes to life with the soft glow of dawn, I find myself working alongside Kofi, the village elder whose patience seems as enduring as the land itself. Today, he teaches me the intricate dance of planting maize, his hands guiding mine through the rich, dark soil. "Like this, Tuoma," he says, a gentle firmness in his voice, his eyes reflecting a mix of kindness and something else — perhaps pity or understanding. I nod, trying to mirror his actions, seeking approval not just for the task but for a place in this foreign world.

Kofi's laughter, warm and hearty, breaks through my concentrated effort as my attempts falter, seeds scattering clumsily from my hands. "You have much to learn," he says, but there's no mockery in his tone, only an affectionate amusement. In these moments, I find a semblance of peace, a temporary respite from the relentless questions haunting me. Yet, even as we share this simple connection, a part of me remains detached, floating adrift on a sea of forgotten memories.

As the sun climbs higher, bringing with it the relentless heat, an unexpected laughter bubbles up from within me, surprising even myself. It's a moment of lightness, fleeting but real, contrasting sharply with the persistent fog of confusion. In this moment, with dirt under my fingernails and the sun warming my back, I allow myself a brief respite from the turmoil within. Later, as the village gathers around the evening fire, I sit beside Ama, the young woman who found me unconscious at the edge of the forest. She speaks softly, her voice a soothing melody, recounting stories of the village — tales of joy, hardship, and the relentless passage of time. I listen, captivated not just by the stories but by the sense of belonging they weave around the listeners. "Tuoma," she turns to me, her gaze locking onto mine, "you are part of our story now." Her words are meant to comfort, yet they echo with a haunting reminder of my own lost narrative.

Every day, the mystery woman's face is there, a ghost in my thoughts, haunting yet comforting. Who is she? My sister, my friend... or someone more? I talk to myself, to her image in my mind, asking questions that hang unanswered in the air. "Who are you?" I whisper at night, but only the silent darkness responds. The villagers see my distant stares, my furrowed brows. "Tuoma thinks too much," they say, not understanding the battle inside me. I smile, nod, but inside, I'm screaming for answers, for memories just out of reach.

It's the nights when thoughts of my mystery woman are most prevalent. I dream. In the dream, I'm wandering through an endless gallery, its walls adorned with paintings that seem familiar yet unreachable. Each piece is a fragment of a memory, a moment suspended in color and light, but they're all incomplete, like parts of a story left untold. I'm drawn to one painting in particular, a near-finished portrait of a woman, her eyes a mix of warmth and sorrow. As I reach out, desperate to connect, the image dissolves under my touch, leaving me in a void, her face the last to fade, intensifying the ache in my heart for the love and life slipping away from my grasp. One morning, while I'm helping fix a roof for one of the elderly villagers, a soldier strolls into our village. There's no panic or fear from anyone; they're used to soldiers passing through. They greet him like they greet any traveler, with curiosity but kindness. His uniform looks familiar, like something from a dream, but no specific memories come to mind. I head to the hut I share with other men, unsure why my heart beats faster at the sight of him.

As I walk past, the soldier stops short and blurts out, "Sergeant Cooper?" I freeze, turning to him, a mix of confusion and recognition crossing my face. He looks shocked to see me, stepping closer as he introduces himself as Private Mitchell.

The surprise in his eyes mirrors my own, a sudden spark of hope igniting within me. Maybe, just maybe, this man holds the key to unlocking the shadows of my past.

I start to tell him about the little I do remember. It's not much, just bits and pieces of life before the jungle. There's a strange sense of relief washing over me, telling someone who might understand who I am. My words are hesitant, broken, but he listens intently, trying to piece together the puzzle of my past.

Private Mitchell explains everything to me in simple terms. He talks about the rescue mission we were on, how there was an explosion, and in the chaos, they couldn't find me. He tells me they've been searching for months, thinking I was lost or worse. And all this time, I've been living here, with no memory of any of it. Hearing this, I'm filled with so many emotions: shock, confusion, but also a strange relief to finally know some of my story.

After that, everything started moving fast. People were planning how to get me back home to the States so doctors could look at me and help me remember everything. But through all this, I couldn't stop thinking about the woman who kept appearing in my thoughts. I knew I had to find out who I was to understand her place in my life. The urgency wasn't just about getting back to familiar surroundings but about unraveling the mystery of her and what we meant to each other.

***

As the plane's engines roar to life, a mix of relief and confusion washes over me. I'm leaving behind a village that became an unexpected refuge, stepping into a metal bird that's supposed to take me 'home'. The seat feels alien under me, too soft, too structured compared to the hard ground I've gotten used to. Outside, the world blurs into motion, and as we ascend, my heart races—not from fear, but from the overwhelming uncertainty of what lies ahead. The familiar yet foreign hum of the aircraft fills my ears, a stark contrast to the quiet life I'm leaving behind. My thoughts keep drifting to the woman, her image a persistent echo in my mind, a reminder of a life I can't fully grasp.

The shift back to the regimented world of Camp LeJeune brings a jarring sense of displacement. The stark military lines and the crisp salutes are a language I once spoke fluently, now reduced to muffled echoes. As Sergeant Harris approaches, confidence emanating from his stride, a spark of envy ignites within me, a longing for the assuredness I once possessed.

"Sergeant Cooper, we've been expecting you," he greets me, his hand extended, a gesture of camaraderie I remember only by the weight of its expectation. I return the handshake, the firmness of his grip a silent reminder of the strength I once possessed.

In the debriefing room, the cold, clinical space envelops me, each officer's uniform a trigger to a life I can't recall. Lieutenant Ford, a man whose face tells stories of countless battles, tries to bridge the gap, his voice a mix of authority and concern. "We're here to help you, Shane," he insists, laying out photographs like breadcrumbs leading back to a past I can no longer taste. I stare at the images, willing recognition to surface, but they remain as lifeless as a painter's discarded sketches.

"Remember this operation?" he probes, pointing to a blurred image of men I should know. My response is a shake of the head, a gesture becoming too familiar, too automatic. The disappointment in his eyes is palpable, a reflection of my own failure mirrored back at me.

Private Mitchell stands in the corner, the bridge between my two worlds. His presence is a comfort, a link to the days lost in the jungle's embrace. After the formalities, he walks me through the barracks, his words a lifeline thrown across the chasm of my lost memories. "You led us through worse than this," he says, a note of reverence in his voice that feels undeserved. "You can get through this too."

The revelation from Private Mitchell, a lifeline thrown into the turbulent waters of my memory, ignites a different kind of shift. The pieces of my past, though fragmented, begin to form a picture, incomplete but beckoning. There's a surge of hope, alien and sweet, contrasting sharply with the despair that's been my constant companion. Another officer, younger, with sympathetic eyes, tries a different approach, showing pictures of a team, my team they tell me, hoping for a spark of recognition. Their names, their faces - they expect me to remember, to connect, but each image triggers a pulse of anxiety rather than clarity. I should know these men, my brothers in arms, but they're strangers to me now. The room suddenly feels even smaller, the walls inching closer, a sensation I remember from nights spent in cramped, unsafe shelters.

As the officers continue to press, each failed attempt to recognize a face or place tightens the knot of frustration in my chest, a sensation mingling with an all-too-familiar sense of panic. My heart races, not just with the desperation to remember but with the echoes of a fear I can't place. My breaths come quicker, shallower, a response I've learned to dread. I'm here, safe, they tell me, but my body reacts as if I'm not, as if the danger is imminent.

My mind races, desperate to grasp the elusive threads of my past, but they slip away, leaving me feeling more isolated, more cut off from the man I'm supposed to be. This disconnect is a constant reminder of what's missing — not just my memory, but the connection to her, the woman whose presence in my mind is my only certainty. Each time I try to focus, a loud noise or a sudden movement jolts me back to a place of fear, a reflex I can't seem to shake off. It's more than confusion; it's a visceral reaction, a body memory of threats and survival.

Her absence in these photos, in these fragments they lay before me, only amplifies the void, making me feel not just lost from myself, but from the love I believe we shared. The sense of loss is overwhelming, not just for the memories I can't reclaim but for the warmth and safety I sense she represented. In this sterile room, surrounded by indifferent walls and expectant faces, her image is a beacon of peace, a stark contrast to the chaos brewing inside me.

The officers' voices fade into the background as another wave of disorientation hits me. I close my eyes for a moment, trying to anchor myself back to the present, away from the invisible threats my mind conjures. I remind myself I'm in a debriefing room, not a war zone, but the distinction blurs under the weight of unseen battles. It's clear they don't understand; they see a soldier who should respond, recover, remember. But I'm a man adrift in a sea of uncharted emotions, grappling with shadows that don't respect the boundaries between past and present.

In the grueling journey of rehabilitation, I can sense the doctors' concern escalating as they confront my persistent frustration and stagnant progress. They start with basic memory exercises, presenting me with simple prompts and questions, their faces marked by increasing worry as I meet their efforts with vacant stares, the remnants of my past just out of reach.

As we advance to sensory therapies, their hope seems to dim alongside my lack of response. Familiar smells and sounds, meant to trigger memories, only seem to deepen the void, drawing reactions from me that range from sheer apathy to quiet panic.

Their concern deepens as they guide me through old photographs, each chosen to spark some flicker of recognition. Yet, each narrative they share meets with silence, amplifying the silent alarm that seems to resonate louder with each failed attempt. They look over at each other, concern creasing their brows as they sift through my military records, which feel as distant and unrelatable to me as a stranger's diary.

Despite their professionalism and years of experience, their strategies fall short. My frustration mirrors theirs, as the divide between who I was and who I am now widens into a seemingly insurmountable gap. In their private discussions, I know they're grappling with the severity of my PTSD, debating over their methods, all the while noting my detached stares, my startle at unexpected noises, my retreat into myself – all indicators of a trauma that goes beyond mere memory loss.

I find myself an outsider in my own recovery, observing their mounting anxiety reflected in subdued conversations and fleeting glances. Their increasing concern only amplifies my isolation, fueling a despair that threatens to engulf me, leaving me to wonder if my very essence, and the fragments of love I strain to remember, are drifting further out of reach with each day that fades.

After weeks of sessions that lead nowhere, the doctors finally offer a different path. They suggest, with cautious optimism, that returning to Macon might spark something inside me. The word 'Macon' echoes like a distant bell in a fog – familiar yet so out of reach. My stomach knots at the thought, tangled in a web of what-ifs and maybes. The prospect of returning to a place I should call home, yet feels as alien as any foreign land, sends a shiver down my spine.

The fear is real, touchable; a dense fog in my mind, making me question everything. What if Macon is just another dead end? What if the faces of family and friends bring no more recognition than the strangers here? But amidst the whirlwind of fear, a tiny strand of hope persists. The mysterious woman who haunts my dreams – could Macon hold the key to her identity? To our story?

Feeling torn inside is hard. I'm stuck feeling sad about how things are now but, maybe, also a bit hopeful that going back to Macon might help. Thinking about walking around places I used to know but can't remember is alarming, but it's like holding onto a small hope. I'm scared of staying lost like this, not knowing who I am. Going to Macon is frightening too, full of things I don't know or remember. But I have to try; it feels like my only shot at finding out who I used to be and getting my life back.

Awaiting Dawn

Emily

As the calendar pages flip closer to the due date, a quiet tension builds within me. My hand instinctively caresses my belly, feeling the life within, a sweet and painful reminder of Shane. The room, filled with soft shadows, seems too vast, too quiet, echoing the emptiness that his absence has carved within me.

I move through the days on autopilot, each task tinged with a sense of solitude that I can't shake off. Preparing the nursery, folding tiny clothes, attending doctor's appointments—every step I take is a dance of shadows, one where joy is intertwined with a deep, pervasive loneliness. I imagine Shane's laughter filling these silent spaces, his voice overlaying the quiet moments, and my heart aches for what should have been.

The fear is a constant undercurrent, dark and relentless. It's not just the fear of childbirth, of the pain and uncertainty that awaits, but a deeper terror—facing it all without him by my side. Questions plague me, circling like vultures over a barren field. How will I look into our child's eyes and explain the absence of their father? How do I hold onto hope when every day stretches out like an endless road with no sign of his return?

The anticipation of childbirth is overshadowed by the weight of his absence. I find myself tracing the outlines of baby clothes, imagining Shane's hands over mine, a shared moment that exists only in daydreams. My heart aches for him to share in the wonder of our child's first breath, first cry, the irreplaceable milestones that we should witness together.

Yet, in this whirlpool of emotions, a strong color is painted on the canvas of my heart—hope. Hope that Shane will return to us, hope that he will walk through the door, hope that our child will know the warmth of his embrace. It is this hope that steadies my trembling hands, that whispers to me in the stillness to be strong—for myself, for our baby.

Each day of my pregnancy has been a journey marked not just by the growing life inside me, but by the palpable absence of Shane. There were moments, so many of them, that I ached to share with him. Like the first time I felt our baby kick, a gentle flutter that soon grew into confident movements. I lay there, hand pressed to my belly, tears streaming down my face, wishing more than anything that Shane could have felt it too. I imagined his hand over mine, his eyes lighting up with the same wonder and love I felt.

Then there were the ultrasounds, the black and white images that were the first visual proof of our baby. I sat in the dimly lit room, clutching the printouts, tracing the outline of what would soon be our child. How I longed for Shane to be there, whispering guesses about who the baby would look like, his arm wrapped protectively around me. I wanted to see the joy in his eyes, to share the overwhelming emotion of seeing our child for the first time.

I've walked through this pregnancy shadowed by Shane's absence, each milestone a bittersweet reminder of what we're missing together. The nursery preparations, choosing the colors, assembling the crib — tasks I undertook alone, with only my thoughts and the echo of our dreams for company. I found myself talking to him, narrating every step as if he could hear me, as if he was just in the next room and not missing, his whereabouts a haunting mystery.

I've missed his reassurance, his strength. There were nights I lay awake, wrestling with worry and fear, craving the comfort of his voice telling me everything would be okay. I longed for the simple joy of choosing baby names together, of imagining our future as a family. Each decision made in his absence felt like a stone in my heart, a constant reminder of the gap between our hoped-for life and my solitary reality.

Every moment, every missed opportunity to share this journey with Shane, has been etched in my heart, a mosaic of joy and sorrow. I've journaled, written letters to Shane I couldn't send, poured out my thoughts, fears, and dreams onto pages he may never read. It's a record of a journey we were supposed to make together, a chronicle of love, waiting, and hope.

As my due date draws near, the reality that Shane might not be here to welcome our child into the world is a heavy burden. Yet, in the quiet moments, when the night is soft and the world is at rest, I feel a connection, an unbreakable bond between Shane, our baby, and me. It's in these moments that my resolve strengthens. Despite the uncertainty, despite the fear, I know that this baby, our baby, will be loved immeasurably — by me, and in my heart, I believe, by Shane too, wherever he may be. Despite Shane's absence, I talk to the baby about him every day, weaving stories of his kindness, his strength, his love for us. I want our child to know his or her father, to feel connected to him, even in this peculiar silence that has enveloped our lives. It's in these conversations, one-sided though they may be, that I find a semblance of normalcy, a thread of continuity from the life we planned to the unexpected reality we face.

I've also prepared myself, gathering not just material things, but mental and emotional strength. I attend birthing classes alone, surrounded by couples, a stark reminder of what's missing. Yet, I stand tall, focusing on the knowledge and skills I'll need, determined to bring our child into the world with as much love and confidence as I can muster. In these classes, I'm not just Emily, I'm Shane's Emily, carrying forward the love and partnership we share, even in his absence.

My friends and family have rallied around me, their support a buoyant force against the tide of Shane's absence. They help me prepare, offering the strength of their presence, their hands, and their hearts. But when the door closes each evening, and I'm left in the quiet of our home, it's Shane's spirit I lean on, the memories of our love, the promise of our family, that I hold close to carry me through the night.

***

It's a sunny afternoon, the kind that Shane loved, with a soft breeze whispering through the open windows, carrying the scent of blooming flowers and the promise of spring. My friends, a group of women who've become my pillars in Shane's absence, have transformed my living room into a sea of pastels and laughter for the baby shower. Balloons dance on the ceiling, tables are adorned with delicate decorations, and there's a warmth that fills the room, a stark contrast to the cold absence in my heart.

As guests start arriving, bearing gifts wrapped in shimmering paper and wide smiles, a wave of gratitude washes over me. Their presence, their care, acts as a temporary balm to my aching soul. Yet, with each hug, each "Congratulations," the absence of Shane's strong arms around me, his voice joining in the chorus of well-wishes, grows more pronounced. I plaster a smile on my face, the mask of the expectant mother thrilled by her upcoming arrival, while inside, a part of me crumbles at the thought of him missing these moments.

My mother, always my anchor in the storm, stands by my side, her hand gently squeezing mine, a silent message of support and shared sorrow. Her eyes, mirrors of my own, reflect an understanding born of her own trials, a testament to the strength she's passed on to me. She leans in, whispering words of encouragement, "You're stronger than you know, Emily. Shane would be so proud." Her words are meant to comfort, but they also twist a knife of longing — for Shane, for normalcy, for a future that seems stolen from us.

Lily, my middle sister, tries her best to lift the spirits, cracking jokes, making everyone laugh, her efforts to shield me from sadness as transparent as glass. She's prepared games that have everyone in stitches, lightening the mood, pulling me, even if just for a moment, from the depths of my thoughts. Watching her, I'm touched by her resolve to make this day special for me, a reminder of the unspoken bond between sisters, a bond that not even the deepest of sorrows can tarnish.

As the laughter from Lily's latest joke begins to subside, the room fills with the soft, comfortable chatter of close friends and family. My gaze shifts to Elaine, who has been quietly arranging the mountain of gifts into neat piles. Unlike Lily's vibrant energy, Elaine has always been the more reflective, the steady calm in any storm. Today, her presence is like a quiet anchor in the sea of pastel decorations and jubilant voices.

Elaine looks up, catching my eye, and offers a small, knowing smile. She moves towards me, her approach measured, her eyes reflecting a depth of understanding that words often fail to capture. "It's been quite the day, hasn't it?" she says, her voice low, infused with the warmth only a sister can offer.

"It has," I reply, feeling a lump form in my throat. Elaine, sensing my unspoken feelings, places a gentle hand on my shoulder.

"Emily," she starts, her voice firm yet filled with compassion, "you're doing incredibly well, you know. Shane would be... will be so proud." The careful change from 'would be' to 'will be' doesn't go unnoticed, offering a sliver of hope in the careful wording.

I nod, fighting back tears, grateful for her strength and belief. "I'm trying, Elaine. It just feels so overwhelming at times."

Elaine squeezes my shoulder reassuringly. "I know, Em, I know. But look around you," she gestures to the room filled with friends and the remnants of celebration, "You're not alone in this. We're all here for you, every step of the way. And when Shane returns, he'll step right into the love that never left."

Her words, so full of certainty and support, bolster my wavering spirit. Elaine has always had this way, a strength that doesn't overshadow but rather uplifts those around her.

Just then, Jenna joins us, linking her arm with mine, a physical manifestation of the solidarity Elaine just spoke of.

"She's right, Emily. This baby is already so loved by so many. Shane included, no matter where he is."

The confluence of Jenna's upbeat spirit with Elaine's steady presence envelops me in a cocoon of sisterhood and friendship. For a moment, the burden of Shane's absence lightens, carried on the shoulders of the incredible women around me.

Elaine, with her quiet wisdom, adds, "And this little one," she pauses, resting her hand lightly on my belly, a mirror of my earlier actions, "is going to grow up knowing just how much he or she is loved. By all of us. By you. And by Shane, no matter the distance."

The room is filled with chatter, stories of motherhood, and shared experiences, a tapestry of life and love. As I open gifts, cooing over tiny outfits and soft blankets, my heart swells with love for this unborn child, a love intertwined with an indelible sadness. Each gift, each gesture of kindness, is a reminder of the life growing inside me, a life created with Shane, a beacon of hope in an ocean of uncertainty. As the baby shower winds down, Jenna lingers, helping me clear the remnants of the celebration. Her presence is a quiet comfort, a reminder of the world outside my swirling thoughts.

"Emily, this was beautiful," Jenna says, stacking plates with a gentle clatter. "Everyone's so excited for you... for the baby."

I offer a weary smile, the fatigue of the day pressing down. "Thanks, Jenna. Today meant a lot. I just wish..." My voice trails off, the familiar ache for Shane surfacing.

Jenna reaches out, her touch light on my arm. "He'll be part of this, Emily. In every story you tell, in every smile of your child. Shane's here, in the love you carry."

Her words, meant to comfort, spark something within me—a flicker of determination amidst the uncertainty. "You're right," I affirm, straightening my shoulders. "I'll make sure our baby knows his or her father, through the stories, through the love he left behind."

Jenna nods, her eyes glistening with unshed tears. "And you're not alone, Emily. We're all here for you, every step of the way."

The sincerity in her words bolsters my spirits. Despite the gaping absence Shane has left, the support of friends like Jenna weaves a safety net around my fraying edges.

Later that evening, my mother and sisters help me sort through the gifts, their laughter a soothing balm to my worn heart. Lily, ever the optimist, holds up a tiny onesie. "Look, Em, future soccer star!" she exclaims, her enthusiasm infectious.

I can't help but laugh, the sound surprising even me. "Shane would love that," I say, allowing the moment of joy to permeate the lingering sadness. "He always talked about teaching our kid to play soccer."

My mother watches me, her eyes soft. "He's still teaching him, in a way," she says softly. "Through you."

Her words resonate deeply, affirming the role I must play for our child. In that moment, surrounded by my family, I feel a surge of strength. I'm not just carrying Shane's child; I'm carrying his legacy, our dreams, and the love we shared. I'm more than just the bearer of our child; I'm the link between past and future, between Shane and the life growing inside me.

"Mom, you're right," I acknowledge, feeling a newfound resolve. "I'll be the voice that tells Shane's stories, the hands that hold our child with his love. I'll be enough for both of us, until he comes home."

The room falls silent, the weight of my words hanging in the air. My sisters nod, their faces a mix of admiration and concern, understanding the journey ahead is mine to walk, yet reminding me I won't have to walk it alone.

As the night draws to a close, and the comforting chaos of family and friends dissipates, I'm left in the quiet of the nursery. The room, once a symbol of Shane's absence, now holds a different meaning. It's proof of the strength I've found within myself, the support of those who love me, and the unbreakable bond between Shane and me, preserved for our child.

I run my fingers over the crib's smooth edge, the unfinished projects, and the new gifts, each a symbol of life continuing, moving forward. In this room, I make a silent promise to my unborn child and to Shane: to be strong, to love fiercely, and to keep hope alive, no matter the distance, no matter the silence.

Awakening Memories

Shane

As I pull up to the old, familiar yet unrecognizable house, a wave of unease washes over me. This is supposed to be my family home, my home, but it feels like stepping onto a movie set—a place designed to mimic life but devoid of personal connection. The lawn, the porch, even the welcome mat, they all seem like artifacts from someone else's history.

I push the door open, half expecting memories to flood back, but they don't. The silence of the house is stifling, filled with the ghosts of laughter and arguments I can't quite grasp. I wander from room to room, touching old furniture, looking at faded photographs, hoping for a spark, a flicker of recognition, but finding none.

It's not until I reach the living room that something shifts. The space is filled with remnants of a life I should remember, each piece a silent testimony to moments lost to me. But it's the piano, sitting unassumingly in the corner, that catches my breath—a dusty, silent guardian of the past. My steps towards it are tentative, each footfall stirring a cloud of forgotten days.

As I stand before it, the urge to touch it, to let my fingers dance on the ivory keys, grows irresistible. I sit, the bench creaking softly under my weight, a familiar yet alien sound. My fingers hover over the keys, and without thinking, I start to play. It's clumsy at first, notes jumbled and uncertain. But then, like a stream finding its course, the melody emerges—hesitant at first, then growing more confident. It's a lullaby, one that seems to seep from the very depths of my soul, a melody my gramma used to play to lull me to sleep, to soothe my childhood fears.

The music fills the room, wrapping around me like a comforting embrace from the past. The notes unlock something inside me, a sliver of warmth in the cold expanse of my amnesia. With each chord, memories start to flicker, shy and fleeting, like fireflies in the night. There's a sense of love, of safety, intertwined with the melody—a reminder of times when life was simpler, when my biggest worry was the monsters under my bed, not the missing pieces of my own story.

This unexpected connection, this bridge to my past, ignites a spark of hope in the darkness of my forgotten life. The melody, so tender and familiar, becomes a beacon, guiding me back to myself, to the person I was before the world turned upside down. It's not much, this fragile thread tethered to a long-lost past, but it's something—a starting point in the daunting journey to reclaim my identity.

With the final note hanging in the air, I sit in silence, letting the echoes of the music wash over me. The excitement of recognition, even if just for a melody, a fragment of my former life, is overwhelming. It's a victory, however small, against the void that has claimed my memories. For the first time since waking in that foreign land, I feel a flicker of hope, a belief that maybe, just maybe, I can find my way back from this limbo. The piano, my gramma's lullaby, has given me a gift—a key to unlock the door to my past, and with it, a chance to rebuild my future.

Days start to blend, each carrying a whisper of familiarity as I find myself drawn, almost magnetically, to the outskirts of town. There, beyond the last row of weathered fences, lies the old fishing hole—a secluded spot cradled by weeping willows, their branches kissing the water's surface. I don't remember the path leading there, but my feet move with purpose, guided by an invisible string tied to my heart.

I don't remember how to tie a hook or bait a line, but sitting by the water's edge feels inexplicably right, like returning to a sacred space forgotten by time. The river, with its gentle, steady flow, speaks a language of peace, whispering secrets I once knew. I close my eyes, and there it is—the echo of laughter, rich and uninhibited, the kind shared between a boy and his granddad on lazy summer afternoons.

Fragments of memories start to bubble to the surface, fragmented and fleeting, but undeniably real. I can almost feel the weight of a fish tugging on the line, the surge of excitement mingled with the calm of nature. The warmth of the sun on my back, a comforting, steady presence, transports me to days filled with simple joys and the clear, uncomplicated bond between a boy and his mentor.

These glimpses into the past, though brief, are like rays of sunlight piercing through the dense fog of my amnesia. Each memory, though as elusive as smoke, brings a sense of belonging, a reminder of a time when I was whole, when my identity was anchored in the love and lessons shared at this very spot.

The nostalgia is overwhelming, a bittersweet tide that lifts me with its promise and stings with its brevity. But it's a start, a crack in the dam holding back a reservoir of lost time. For a few precious moments, the confusion and frustration that have become my constant companions fade into the background, replaced by the serene certainty of connection to a life that was once mine.

With each visit, the memories grow stronger, more coherent. I begin to embrace these solo excursions as therapy, a self-imposed ritual to stitch the fragments of my past back together. The old fishing hole, with its tranquil waters and whispered memories, becomes my sanctuary, a place where I can slowly rebuild the bridge to my past, one memory at a time.

The nights are the hardest, when the quiet of the house wraps around me like a blanket, too tight, suffocating in its embrace. In these moments, as I drift into sleep, she comes to me, the woman from my dreams, so real and vivid that I can almost touch her. Yet, with every dawn, she slips away, leaving nothing but a hollow ache in her wake.

In these dreams, she's there—always just out of reach, her face obscured by the shadows of my mind or turned away at the last moment. I stretch out my hand, desperate to touch her, to bring her into the clarity of my waking world, but like mist, she slips through my fingers. And then the dream shifts, and I'm no longer in the comfort of imagined arms but on the battlefield, surrounded by chaos, the air thick with the smell of gunpowder and the metallic tang of blood.

I wake from these dreams gasping, as if I've been dragged from one reality to another, leaving pieces of my soul scattered across the landscapes of my mind. The war, a fragmented mosaic of horror and adrenaline, invades the sanctity of my sleep, intertwining with the softer memories of her, creating a tapestry of conflict and longing.

But the frustration that comes is palpable. I can almost hear the melody of the lullaby, feel the dewy grass under my feet, recall the laughter of days gone by, but her — the core of my nightly visions — remains elusive, shrouded in mystery. It's like being thirsty in a sea of saltwater, surrounded by memories that only serve to remind me of what I cannot fully grasp.

Why does she visit me only to vanish with the morning sun? Each time she appears, it feels like a piece of me is being teased, toyed with by my own mind. It's a silent battle, one where the heart knows what the mind cannot fathom. The more I try to chase her through the fog of my amnesia, the more she fades, leaving me grappling with a sense of loss for someone I can't even remember.

I'm tired of the shadows, tired of the chase. Yet, I can't give up. She's the key, I feel it — the key to unlock the door to my past, to understand who I am. But each day that passes without recollection feels like a step further away from her, from me, from the truth. The elusive nature of these memories, like smoke slipping through my fingers, leaves me restless, a wanderer in my own mind.

***

Taking walks becomes my solace, a temporary escape from the confines of a reality that feels both suffocating and surreal. Each step on the river walk brings a mixed sense of familiarity and displacement. The path, bordered by whispering trees and the steady, comforting flow of the river, seems to beckon me towards memories that lie just beneath the surface, like stones beneath clear water.

I wander, lost in thought, the sounds of the water mingling with the rustle of leaves, a symphony that seems to resonate with the rhythm of a past life. It's a strange sensation, like walking through a dream, the kind where you know you belong but can't quite figure out why. The scenic beauty of the river walk, with its serene water and vibrant greens, feels like a backdrop to a play where I'm the lead actor who's forgotten his lines.

I pause, letting the scenes unfold before me, watching families and couples pass by in laughter and conversation. There's a piercing in my heart, a yearning for something, or someone, missing. It's as if each smiling face, each shared moment I witness, is a mirror reflecting back a life that's been erased from my memory. The joy I see feels both uplifting and cruel, a reminder of what I've lost or perhaps never had.

The river, with its relentless flow, becomes a metaphor for my own journey – moving forward, yet with no clear direction, guided by an unseen force, navigating through the fog of forgotten days. There are moments when the sunlight breaks through the canopy, casting glittering reflections on the water, moments of such piercing beauty and clarity that my heart clenches with a mix of joy and sorrow.

It's on this path, amidst the fleeting glimpses of clarity, that I find myself grappling with the shadows of my past. The tranquility of the river walk stands in stark contrast to the turmoil within me. Memories dance frustratingly just out of reach, tantalizing hints of laughter, love, and life before the silence. With each step, the fragments of my past flicker in and out of focus, like leaves fluttering in and out of the sunlight.

Yet, in this place of natural harmony, I find a semblance of peace, a fleeting sense of belonging that soothes the raw edges of my fragmented memories. It's here, amidst the gentle sounds of nature, that I allow myself a momentary respite from the relentless quest to piece together the puzzle of my past. The river walk, with its undemanding presence, offers me a space to breathe, to feel, to exist without the heavy weight of confusion and loss.

But as the walk comes to an end, the tranquility fades, replaced once again by the echo of my own footsteps—a constant reminder that while the journey offers brief moments of escape, the quest for my lost memories continues. It's a path I walk alone, guided by the silent hope that somewhere along this winding river, the answers I seek lie waiting, submerged just below the surface, waiting for the moment they can break free and flood back into the light of day.

One day, almost as if on autopilot, my feet guide me through the quaint streets of downtown, each turn more instinctual than the last. It's a crisp morning, the kind that hints at the change of seasons, a new chapter waiting to unfold. My path leads me to an art gallery, a place that beckons with an invisible string pulling at the corners of my soul.

As I push open the door, a bell chimes softly, announcing my presence in a room filled with color and light. The walls are adorned with paintings that seem to pulse with life, each canvas telling its own silent story. I'm drawn in, wandering between the artworks, each brushstroke and hue whispering secrets to a part of me I thought was lost.

There's a peculiar sense of anticipation that tightens in my chest as I move deeper into the gallery. It's a feeling akin to the moments before awakening from a dream, where reality and fantasy blur, leaving you questioning which world you belong to.

And then, amidst the myriad of colors and shapes, I see her. Across the room, bathed in the soft gallery light, stands the woman from my dreams. She's as real as the art that surrounds us, her presence pulling at the threads of my memory, unraveling the knots that have bound my past.

But something's different—she's pregnant, her figure outlined gracefully against the backdrop of canvases. She's engaged in conversation with a couple, gesturing towards a painting with a familiarity and passion that captivates not just them, but me, from afar. My heart stutters, a tumult of emotions crashing into me with the force of a tidal wave. Joy, confusion, fear—they all mingle in a chaotic dance, leaving me rooted to the spot.

The questions start to flood my mind, each one more pressing than the last. Who is the father? How long have I been gone? What has transpired in the swath of time that remains shrouded in darkness to me? The sight of her, so vivid and vital, contrasts sharply with the fragmented, ethereal images that haunt my dreams.

For a moment, the world narrows to just her and me, separated by the expanse of the gallery yet inexplicably connected. The rest of the room fades away, leaving a tunnel of clarity that pierces through the fog that has enveloped my life. My palms sweat, my throat tightens, and a mix of longing and dread settles heavy in my stomach.

I'm torn between wanting to rush to her side, to confront the reality of her, of us, and the urge to flee, to escape the potential heartbreak that her presence signifies. The mystery of her identity, of our connection, has been the one constant in my nightmarish limbo. Now, faced with the possibility of answers, I'm paralyzed by the weight of what those answers might mean.

The pregnant woman, the living embodiment of my dreams, continues her conversation, unaware of the storm she's ignited within me. My feet are cemented to the gallery floor, my body a battlefield of warring emotions. This moment, suspended between past and future, is a crossroads, the point where the river of my forgotten past blends into the canvas of my present reality. And as I stand there, lost and found all at once, I realize that no matter what truths await me, the journey forward starts with confronting the questions I've been afraid to ask.

She turns, and our eyes lock. Instantly, a whirlwind of emotions plays across her face: recognition, shock, confusion, and something deeper, something like the echo of a shared past. In that single moment, my world shifts on its axis. Emily. The name rushes back to me, gentle yet overwhelming, like a breeze that carries the scent of forgotten flowers.

The memories come crashing in waves, relentless and liberating. Moments we shared flash before my eyes: laughter under the summer sky, whispered confessions in the dead of night, promises made with the naivety of those untouched by the harshness of reality. Each memory is a piece of the puzzle that's been missing, snapping into place with aching clarity.

My heart races, a tumultuous symphony of joy and disbelief. How is it possible? Here she stands, the woman who's haunted my dreams, the anchor in my storm of forgetfulness. But there's more than just joy in this reunion; there's an undercurrent of confusion and fear. She's pregnant, her condition undeniable, a stark reminder of the time that has slipped through my fingers, of the life I've been absent from.

As I stand there, frozen, our eyes meet across the crowded space, bridging months and silence in a single breath. Time, heartless in its march, halts for us, bending to the gravity of this moment. Emily's eyes, wide with disbelief, search mine, seeking the truths hidden behind months of absence.

"Shane?" Her voice breaks the spell, a whisper torn from the depths of a heart long burdened by uncertainty. It's a question, a plea, a tether thrown across the chasm of lost time.

The name, my name, in her voice, unleashes a torrent within me. It's as if she's spoken the incantation needed to break the spell of amnesia that's held me captive. My feet, previously rooted in place by fear and doubt, now carry me to her as if drawn by the most potent magnet.

"Emily." The word is more than just a name; it's a confession, an apology, a prayer. I'm close enough now to see the shimmer of tears in her eyes, the pulse fluttering at the base of her throat, the myriad of emotions playing across her face.

Her next move is hesitant, a step forward that speaks volumes, bridging the gap between past and future. The distance closes, and without a word, she reaches out, her hand trembling as it finds mine. The contact is electric, a shockwave of memories, feelings, and undeniable connection. Her hand in mine is the missing piece, fitting perfectly, grounding me to this moment, to her.

"Shane, is it really you?" Her voice is a blend of hope and heartbreak, echoing the tumultuous journey etched in the lines of her face.

"It's me, Emily," I assure her, my own voice rough with emotion. "I'm so sorry... I..." Words fail me, inadequate to bridge the chasm of missed time, of her pain and my own emptiness.

She searches my face, her gaze intense, seeking the familiar in this stranger before her. "You're here," she whispers, more to herself than to me, a balm soothing the raw edges of her shattered expectations.

The air around us thickens with unspoken words, heavy with the weight of our shared past and the uncertain future. Her other hand, hesitant but driven by a force beyond her control, reaches up to touch my face, as if confirming my presence, grounding herself to the reality that I stand before her.

Tears breach the dam of her eyes, tracing paths of silent sorrow and joy down her cheeks. My own eyes blur, the sight of her pain, my absence reflected in her tears, cutting through the fog that has shrouded my heart.

"Emily, I—" How do you apologize for the lost days, for silent screams in the night, for the uncountable tears shed in the solitude of longing? "I don't remember everything... but I remember you. I can't believe you're here, that you're real."

Her laugh, a soft, disbelieving sound, pierces the heavy air between us. "I've dreamt of this moment," she confesses, her voice thick with tears. "But I never allowed myself to believe it could be real."

Our hands tighten around each other, a lifeline amidst the storm of our emotions. Here, in the eye of our reunion, words are superfluous. Our eyes, our touch, speak the volumes that our lips cannot form.

"I've missed you," I manage to say, the understatement of a lifetime, but the only words that my overwhelmed heart can muster.

"And I, you," she responds, her voice a whisper of resilience, of enduring hope. "But you're here now. You're home."

The word 'home' reverberates between us, a concept so foreign yet desperately coveted. Home isn't just a place; it's this moment, her hand in mine, the silent understanding that no matter how the journey unfolds, it begins and ends with us, together.

As I pull her gently into an embrace, the world falls away, leaving only the reality of her in my arms. Her body fits against mine with a familiarity that belies the months lost, a testament to the enduring bond that not even time could sever. In her embrace, I find the missing pieces of myself, the anchor I've unknowingly sought through the fog of lost memories.

Reclaimed Horizons

Emily

The air in my living room felt thick, charged with a silence too profound for mere words. The soft ticking of the wall clock sounded like a drumbeat, marking the seconds that stretched between Shane and me like years. Outside, the setting sun cast long shadows across the room, painting a picture of a life that had once been vibrant and full of color.

Shane stood awkwardly by the door, a stranger in the very space that had echoed with our shared laughter and whispered dreams. His eyes, once the beacon of my existence, now searched the room, landing on familiar objects, trying to find an anchor in the storm of our shattered past.

I wrapped my arms around myself, a feeble attempt to shield my heart from the flood of emotions threatening to break through my carefully constructed barriers. The joy of seeing him was a tumultuous wave, crashing into the beach of reality, eroded by months of pain and unanswered questions.

"We should sit," I murmured, my voice a ghost of its former self. The couch, a silent witness to our past, now felt like a chasm separating us. As Shane took a tentative seat, the distance between us wasn't just physical; it was a vast expanse filled with the debris of a life interrupted.

"How have you been, Emily?" His voice broke the silence, a tentative bridge over the chasm.

The question, simple yet impossibly complex, hung in the air. How could I explain the sleepless nights, the endless days filled with aching emptiness, the weight of carrying a life within me that he didn't know existed?

"I've been surviving," I replied, my words laced with an honesty that surprised even me. "It's been... hard."

I watched as his face fell, the shadow of guilt casting a pall over his features. "I can't imagine what I put you through," he said, his words heavy with remorse.

Memories flashed before my eyes - our last morning together, filled with mundane promises and casual goodbyes, not knowing it would be the last. The agony of not knowing where he was, if he was safe, the endless waiting for a call that never came.

"It was the not knowing that was the hardest," I admitted, allowing the truth to seep through the cracks in my facade. "Every day, wondering if you were out there somewhere, if you even remembered me."

Shane reached out, his hand hovering in the space between us before retreating, a physical manifestation of our current reality. "I never stopped thinking about you, Emily. Even when I didn't know who I was, there was this feeling, this sense that something... someone important was missing from my life."

Shane's eyes held a torment that mirrored the chaos of my own heart. "And now, seeing you here, like this..." His gaze dropped to my rounded belly, a silent witness to the life that had grown in his absence. "I can't believe I almost missed this," he whispered, a mix of wonder and anguish coloring his tone.

I got up from the couch and moved over to the kitchen to give me time to digest what was going on. The tea kettle was on the stove so I filled it up and put some water on to boil. There was so much to tell him.

"There's so much you've missed, Shane," I said softly, the words spilling forth like water from a breached dam. "Days turned into weeks, weeks into months... and with each passing moment, the hope of seeing you again started to fade, replaced by the harsh truth of your absence."

Shane came over to me in the kitchen. His hand finally bridged the distance between us, touching mine with a tentative gentleness. The contact sparked a jolt of electricity, a reminder of the connection that, despite everything, refused to be severed.

"I'm sorry, Emily," he said, and in those three words, I heard the depth of his regret, the acknowledgment of the pain we both endured. "I'm sorry for the silence, the unknown... for leaving you alone when you needed me the most."

I looked down at our intertwined hands, a symbol of tentative reconciliation. "But you're here now," I whispered, the reality settling in with a weight all its own. "You're here, and we have to figure out what that means... for us, for our baby."

Shane's gaze met mine, holding a resolve that had been absent when he first stepped into the room. "I want to be here for you, for our child," he declared, the anxiety of his missing time mixing with the determination in his voice. "I may not remember everything from my past, but I know I want to be part of this future, Emily. If you'll let me."

The sincerity in his eyes, the earnestness of his words, chipped away at the walls I had built around my heart. It wasn't going to be easy. But as I looked into Shane's eyes, seeing there the reflection of our shared past and the flicker of our future, I felt a glimmer of hope.

"We have a lot to catch up on," I finally said, a small smile breaking through the turmoil. "And we'll need to prepare, not just for the baby, but for how we navigate everything... together."

Shane nodded, his expression a mixture of gratitude and resolve. "Whatever it takes, Emily. I missed too much already; I don't want to miss a moment more."

My hands, betraying a need for normalcy, moved mechanically to prepare tea, the familiar ritual a stark contrast to the turmoil churning inside me. The act of pouring water, the gentle clink of ceramic, seemed alien, as if performed by someone else—someone untouched by the chaos of lost love and sudden reunions.

Shane moved cautiously, mirroring my steps but maintaining a respectful distance, as if the air between us was a delicate glass pane he feared to shatter. We settled onto the couch, a piece that had been a silent spectator to our shared history, now a neutral ground as we navigated the treacherous waters of reconciliation.

I wrapped my fingers around the warm mug, seeking comfort in its steadiness. "When I found out I was pregnant," I started, my voice steady despite the tempest inside, "you were the first person I wanted to tell." My eyes lifted to meet his, holding within them the weight of solitary days and silent nights. "But you were gone, Shane. And with every passing day, the joy of that discovery was overshadowed by the fear of facing it all without you."

His response was written across his face before he spoke a word, a visage marred by pain and self-reproach. "Emily, I—" He paused, struggling to find words that could possibly bridge the chasm of hurt his disappearance had caused. "I can't imagine the strength it took to go through that alone. I should have been there."

The honesty in his voice, raw and unguarded, stirred something within me—a blend of heartache and a flickering, stubborn flame of what might still be. "It was the not knowing that was the hardest, Shane," I confessed, allowing vulnerability to seep through the cracks of my armor. "Not knowing where you were, if you were safe... if you even remembered me."

His hand tentatively covered mine, a gesture so familiar yet so foreign in the context of our fragmented reality. "There wasn't a moment, even in the depths of confusion, that I didn't feel the absence of something... someone vital. It was you, Emily. Always you."

The touch, meant to comfort, sparked a complex cascade of emotions—anger at the abandonment, sorrow for the shared moments lost, and an undeniable undercurrent of longing for what had once been. The dichotomy of wanting to pull away while simultaneously yearning to lean closer mirrored the conflicting tides of my heart.

"In those moments of uncertainty," I continued, "I held onto the memories of us, clinging to the hope that somehow, they'd lead you back to me." My voice wavered, the dam holding back months of solitude and silent battles beginning to crack.

Shane's gaze held mine, a silent plea for forgiveness lingering in the depths of his eyes. "I'm here now, Emily. I know I have a lifetime of moments to make up for, and I know sorry will never be enough. But I'm here, and I'm not going anywhere. I want to be a part of this, of everything." His voice was firm, underscored by a resolute earnestness that spoke of his commitment to the future, our future.

"Talk to me, Shane. What happened to you?" I asked, my voice stronger than I felt.

He took a deep breath, his eyes anchoring to the mug as if it were a lifeline. "It's all so fragmented," he began, his voice a mixture of confusion and fear. "There are days I wake up not recognizing where I am, haunted by nightmares I can't understand. They told me... they told me I was found wandering, no ID, nothing. There are holes in my memory, gaps where months... years should be."

I listened, the anger that had simmered inside me cooling with each word. The man before me was broken, a shadow of the vibrant soul he once was. "I see you in my dreams, Emily, and in my waking moments, but it's like looking through shattered glass. I feel this ache, this profound loss, but when I try to grasp the memories, they slip away."

He looked up, his eyes meeting mine, raw with vulnerability. "I fought to come back, even when I didn't know who or where 'back' was. The pain, the confusion... it doesn't excuse my absence, but I need you to know I never chose to leave you."

My heart clenched at the sheer agony etched across his face. The resentment I had harbored, the nights I cursed his name for leaving me alone, began to dissolve in the wake of his torment. This man, the love of my life, was lost, fighting battles he couldn't remember against an enemy he couldn't see.

"Shane," I said softly, closing the distance between us, compelled by a force beyond my anger, "I can't pretend to understand what you're going through. I was angry, so angry and hurt, but seeing you now, hearing this... I can't hold on to that anger."

He reached out, his hand tentatively cupping my cheek, a touch so full of longing and regret. "I'm so sorry, Emily. For everything you had to go through alone, for not being there when you needed me most."

A solitary tear escaped, breaking through the dam I had meticulously constructed around my heart. His thumb, gentle and hesitant, caught the tear, his touch a bittersweet reminder of what we once had. The warmth from his skin seemed to seep into my very bones, reigniting long-dormant embers.

"You're incredible, Emily," he whispered, his voice hoarse with emotion. "I don't know if I deserve another chance, but I want to be here—for you, for our child. I want to face everything, all of it, together."

The sincerity in his words, the familiar warmth of his touch, broke down the remnants of my defenses. He was here, flawed and broken, yet sincere and hopeful. I looked into his eyes, seeing the man I'd loved, the one I'd lost, and now, unbelievably, had found again.

Without a word, I leaned into him, closing the gap between past pain and present forgiveness. His breath hitched as our faces drew closer, the months apart melting away in the few inches that still separated us. Then, softly, our lips met, a tentative touch that spoke volumes, a kiss imbued with the sorrow of our separation and the flickering hope of our reconnection.

The space between us, before filled with tension and unspoken regrets, now pulsed with a renewed energy, a magnetic pull drawing us irrevocably together. Our kiss, initially soft and tentative, deepened into something more urgent, more desperate—a silent communication of our mutual longing and the pain of our prolonged separation.

His hands, once hesitant, now roamed with purpose over the contours of my back, tracing paths that reignited old flames, stirring emotions I thought were lost to the past. I responded in kind, my fingers weaving through his hair, pulling him closer, as if trying to meld his soul with mine.

Breaking away from the kiss, we looked into each other's eyes, seeing the reflection of our own raw, unguarded selves. In that moment, the world with all its chaos and uncertainty faded away, leaving only the truth of our shared heartbeat, the undeniable reality of our connection.

"Stay with me tonight," I whispered, my voice a blend of desire and certainty. It was not a question, but an invitation—a need to explore this renewed bond, to affirm our connection not just in words and promises, but through the union of our bodies and souls.

Shane's answer was in his eyes before he voiced it out loud. "Nothing I want more," he breathed, his words sealing the silent vow we had made. His hands, strong yet gentle, guided me toward the bedroom, our sanctuary from the world's prying eyes, a place where we could rediscover each other, where we could heal.

The familiar yet now electrifying touch of our skin, the shared breaths, the quiet undressing—all felt like rituals, sacred acts of reclamation and reunion. Every kiss, every touch, was both a rediscovery of old territories and an exploration of new landscapes shaped by the trials we had endured apart.

In the dim light of the bedroom, our bodies found a rhythm as old as time yet as fresh as the new life we were about to welcome. The world outside our embrace ceased to exist as we moved together, guided by a force more potent than either of us could have imagined.

That night, we did not just share our bodies; we shared our fears, our dreams, and our unwavering resolve to face whatever the future held—together. It was a reclamation of lost time, a celebration of our enduring love, and a testament to the strength we found in each other.

As we lay entwined in the aftermath, the gentle rise and fall of our chests syncing in the quiet of the night, I felt a peace I hadn't known in months. The journey ahead would undoubtedly be fraught with challenges, but as I drifted off to sleep, wrapped in Shane's embrace, I knew we were ready to face them—together. In that moment, the fragments of our past and the uncertainty of our future wove together, forming the tapestry of a new beginning, crafted in love, resilience, and a shared hope for the days to come.

The following morning, I stirred, finding Shane's arms still wrapped around me, a protective cocoon that had shielded us through the night. His breathing was even, peaceful, but the tension from the previous day's revelations still lingered in the air, unspoken but palpable.

As Shane woke, his eyes met mine, and I saw the flicker of yesterday's turmoil replaced by a quiet resolve. We lingered in silence, a shared understanding that today was not just another day; it was the beginning of our journey back to each other, and forward, into the unknown terrain of our future together.

In the kitchen, the mundane act of cooking breakfast together felt different, imbued with a new sense of intimacy and partnership. Shane broke the comfortable silence, his voice hesitant but determined. "Emily, I need to talk to you about something important," he started, pausing as if gathering the strength to continue.

I turned off the stove, giving him my full attention, bracing myself for what was to come. He took a deep breath, his eyes searching mine for understanding before he continued. "I've been struggling with PTSD since I came back," he admitted, the words seeming to cost him with every syllable.

My heart clenched, not out of fear, but from the pain of knowing he had been suffering, silently battling demons I couldn't see. "I keep reliving moments I don't fully understand, flashes of fear, confusion, and loss," Shane confessed, his voice faltering. "It's like being trapped in a loop, with memories that aren't fully mine, shadows of a past I can't piece together."

I reached out, taking his hand, a silent encouragement for him to continue. "I want to be here for you and our baby, more than anything," he said, squeezing my hand as if drawing strength from our connection. "But I know I need help, to confront this, to be the partner and father you both deserve."

Tears pricked my eyes, not just for the pain he was enduring, but for the immense love and courage it took for him to admit his vulnerabilities. "Shane, I'm here for you, just like you're here for us," I assured him, my voice steady despite the emotional turmoil inside. "We'll get through this together."

He nodded, a sense of relief crossing his features, as if a burden had been lifted by sharing his truth. "I've been looking into therapy, support groups for veterans with PTSD," he continued, a proactive edge to his words now. "I'm determined to face this, not just for me, but for us, for our family."

My heart swelled with a mixture of pride, love, and renewed hope. Here was the man I fell in love with, not diminished by his struggles, but standing stronger in the face of them, ready to fight for a better future, not just for himself, but for all of us.

We spent the day reminiscing, walking along the Ocmulgee River, the site of so many of our early memories. The Cherry Blossom Festival was in full swing, the park alive with vibrant colors, art, and the laughter of families. It was a bittersweet experience, walking among the celebration of life and renewal, knowing the silent battles Shane was fighting within.

Yet, as we talked about our hopes and dreams, sampled foods from various stalls, and wandered through the art displays, there was an underlying current of strength and resilience. Shane's openness about his PTSD, his commitment to healing and to our family, infused me with an unexpected sense of optimism.

Later, I took him to The Art Gallery, the dream I had nurtured into reality during his absence. As I shared my aspirations for the gallery, my plans to create a space that combined art therapy and community support, I saw a new light in Shane's eyes—an inspired spark kindled by the possibility of contributing, of being part of something meaningful.

Standing there, surrounded by the tangible results of my own dreams, listening to Shane share his aspirations to be a good father and partner, and his commitment to addressing his

PTSD, I felt a profound shift in our dynamic. It was as if we were building a new foundation, one forged from the remnants of our past and the strength of our present commitment.

The day, marked by openness and shared dreams, ended with a quiet dinner at home, a simple yet profound affirmation of the life we were rebuilding together. As night fell, and we settled in, the challenges ahead seemed less daunting, for in sharing our vulnerabilities, we had discovered a new depth to our love and a renewed commitment to face whatever lay ahead—together.

A month had passed since that profound evening, with each day adding to the mural of our rekindled relationship. We had moved into Shane's family old home, transforming it piece by piece into our own sanctuary. One of the bedrooms, now awash with soft hues of blues and greens, mirrored the one in my studio, soon to be our baby's room. The transformation was more than just cosmetic; it was symbolic, a physical manifestation of our building future and mending pasts.

Shane had been attending therapy sessions at the VA hospital in Milledgeville, a commitment he approached with the same determination he had once reserved for his military duties. I saw the changes in him, subtle but significant. The haunted look that had shadowed his features was gradually being replaced by a clarity, a presentness that had been missing since his return.

It was a Sunday morning when unexpected pains started to knot my belly. At first, I brushed them off as normal discomforts of late pregnancy, not wanting to alarm Shane or admit to myself that something might be wrong. But as the day progressed, the intervals between the pains shortened, the discomfort turning into a pronounced, rhythmic ache.

"Em, what's wrong?" Shane's voice cut through my haze of denial, his eyes reflecting a mix of concern and fear.

"It's nothing," I lied, attempting to mask the pain with a forced smile. "Just some aches, probably moved too fast."

But the facade crumbled quickly under the weight of undeniable pain, the intervals growing closer, the discomfort sharpening. "Shane, I think... I think it might be time," I admitted, the reality settling in with a weight all its own. The baby was coming, and it was a month early.

Panic flickered briefly in Shane's eyes, replaced swiftly by the resolve that had become his new armor. "Okay, okay, let's get you to the hospital," he said, his voice calm but filled with urgency.

The drive to the hospital was a blur, my mind grappling with the rapid onset of labor, overshadowed by the fear for our baby's wellbeing. Shane's hand found mine, a steady presence amidst the swirling chaos, his reassurances a lifeline as we navigated the uncertain waters of early labor.

At the hospital, time seemed to fold in on itself, hours blending into moments filled with whispered words of encouragement, the clasp of hands, and shared glances of hope and fear. Shane was my rock, a constant presence by my side, his own fears for our baby's early arrival swallowed by his unwavering support for me.

In the early hours of the morning, as dawn's light began to seep through the hospital curtains, our baby boy, Atticus Shane, was brought into the world. His first cry pierced the silence, a sound filled with the fresh promise of life, echoing the overwhelming relief and boundless love enveloping the room. As the nurses gently placed Atticus into my arms, the reality of our son, so fiercely wanted and lovingly anticipated, settled around us like a warm blanket.

Atticus, a delicate name chosen with love and reverence, honored the legacy of our grandfathers – my own, known for his wisdom and kindness, and Shane's, remembered for his strength and resilience. In our son, these virtues seemed already whispered, a silent pledge carried on his tiny breaths.

He was small, the result of arriving a month early, each feature on his face meticulously crafted. His eyes, when they fluttered open briefly, held the spark of curiosity and innocence, gazing into the new world with wonder. Despite his size, there was a palpable strength in his grip as he wrapped his tiny fingers around mine, a silent, powerful bond forming in that tender clasp.

However, the joy of Atticus's arrival was tempered by the reality of his prematurity. The doctors, with gentle voices and reassuring smiles, explained that he needed to stay in the neonatal intensive care unit to gain more weight before we could take him home. Though my heart ached at the thought of leaving the hospital without him, I found solace in the knowledge that he was active and healthy, his tiny chest rising and falling with the vigor of a fighter, his movements full of newborn determination.

Shane stood by my side, a silent pillar of strength, his hand never leaving mine as we watched over Atticus. His eyes, filled with a mix of awe and concern, never strayed far from our son, watching every breath, every small movement with a protective gaze. In those quiet, reflective moments by Atticus's side, I saw not just the man I loved, but the father he had become, his love for our son a fierce flame burning in his eyes.

The two weeks in the hospital stretched out, each day a mixture of anxious waiting and quiet moments of bonding. Shane and I took turns holding Atticus, whispering stories of our lives, our hopes, and dreams for his future, painting a tapestry of words for him to grow into. We introduced him to the sound of our voices, the touch of our hands, imprinting ourselves in his new world, a foundation of love for him to build upon.

Atticus Shane, our beautiful boy, was a beacon of new beginnings. His presence, so small yet so profound, had already begun to heal old wounds, weaving a new story from the frayed threads of our past. As we prepared to bring him home, ready to embark on this new journey as a family, I knew that no matter what challenges lay ahead, the love that had brought us to this point – that had brought Atticus into our lives – would guide us through anything.

In the sanctuary of Shane's family home, now reborn as our own, we awaited the day we could finally bring Atticus home. The room we had prepared for him, bathed in soft blues and greens, awaited its occupant with quiet anticipation. And as Shane and I stood together, united in our love for our son and for each other, we stepped into the future not as individuals, but as a family, forever changed, forever grateful, and forever bound by the love we shared for our son, Atticus Shane.

When we were finally able to bring Atticus, affectionately known as Atty, the days following were a blend of sleepless nights and quiet moments of awe, watching the rise and fall of our baby's chest, memorizing every tiny feature. Shane, ever the protective father, hovered with a mix of reverence and nervousness, his love for our child a tangible force that filled the room.

In those quiet, early days of parenthood, amidst the exhaustion and overwhelming love, we found a new rhythm, a new normal that was uniquely ours. The challenges of Shane's PTSD, the shadows of our past hardships, didn't disappear, but they were tempered by the bond we shared and the life we had created together.

As we navigated this new chapter, the fears and uncertainties of the future lingered, but they were overshadowed by the strength of our love—a love that had weathered the deepest storms and emerged not unscathed, but stronger, more resilient, and more profound.

New Beginnings, Shared Dreams

Shane

I wake early. Military training still controlling my sleep habits. I lie still for a moment, letting the reality of my new life seep in. The steady breath of Emily beside me, the soft murmur of Atty from the next room, they're reminders of how much has changed, how much I've changed.

The shadows of the past, once my constant companions, have started to recede, replaced by the tangible, vibrant presence of my family. It's a shift I feel deep in my bones, a grounding force amid the turbulence of readjusting to civilian life and dealing with PTSD.

Rising quietly, I make my way to Atty's room. He's awake, 'Da da", his little hands reaching up when he sees me, a toothless smile spreading across his face. The world narrows down to this moment, to the undeniable bond between father and son. I lift him, feeling the solid weight of his trust and love, and in this quiet hour, I find a peace I once thought lost forever.

In the kitchen, the rhythm of our morning unfolds with practiced ease. Emily joins us, her hair tousled from sleep, her eyes lighting up as she sees us. The domestic scene would have seemed alien to me a year ago, but now it's my anchor, a testament to the life we're building together.

While I prepare breakfast, Emily feeds Atty, her voice a soft melody of coos and murmurs. We move around each other in a comfortable dance, a harmony born of shared responsibilities and mutual respect. The scent of coffee blends with the warmth of the morning sun, crafting a simple yet profound sense of contentment.

As we sit down to eat, the three of us together, I can't help but reflect on the journey that brought us here. The road was long and fraught with shadows, but as I look across the table at Emily and down at Atty in his high chair, I know every step was worth it. This is what healing looks like, what love feels like.

In the quiet kitchen, the air between Emily and me vibrates with an unspoken understanding. She leans in, a movement filled with the familiarity and warmth that has grown between us, her eyes reflecting a shared longing. Our lives, so intertwined with responsibility and care, sometimes whisper for these moments of stolen intimacy.

As our lips meet, the world outside our little bubble fades, replaced by the heat of shared breaths and the quiet urgency of need suppressed by nights of broken sleep and days filled with the laughter and cries of our son. The kiss deepens, a silent language of love and want that speaks of the depth of our connection, of the journey we've traveled together, and the roads still to explore.

But as quickly as the flame ignites, it's quenched by a small, insistent voice, shattering our sanctuary of warmth and intimacy. "Mama! Dada!" Atty's call, imbued with the innocence and immediacy only a child possesses, echoes through our home, a stark reminder of the world beyond us.

We part, our breaths mingling for a fleeting second longer, sharing a smile that speaks volumes—of love, of frustration, of the reality of our new life. Emily's eyes, alight with the fire that I've come to know and cherish, hold mine. "Later," she murmurs, her voice a velvet promise, laden with the anticipation of unfinished business, of desires deferred but not forgotten.

I nod, the promise of later igniting a spark of anticipation, a beacon through the routine of our day. We turn towards our son, stepping back into the roles life has entrusted us with, but the promise hangs in the air, a sweet note of anticipation, of shared secrets and shared lives.

The day unfolds, each moment a step towards 'later', the normalcy of our life as parents interlaced with silent glances and soft touches, reminders of the promise we've made. And as Atty's energy finally wanes and he succumbs to his afternoon nap, the promise of our morning's interrupted kiss pulls us back to each other, a silent acknowledgment of the passion that simmers, undimmed, beneath the surface of our daily lives.

***

Emily lands with a bounce where I dropped her on the bed. I got to work feverishly undoing the buttons on her blouse. I was dying to touch and taste what was underneath. Climbing to my knees on the bed, I pushed the blouse off her delicate shoulders and exposed the beautiful rounded mounds I had been thinking about all day.

My hands roamed over them, cupping them in my hands and pinching the nipples until they were peaked and tight. I leaned down to suck on them, hearing her groans of pleasure. My desire took over. I wanted the heat of her body pressed against me. I reached for her belt as she raised her hips to greet me. I removed her belt and her pants. My hardness was growing with the need of her.

"I want you, Emily." When she opened her mouth to answer, I pressed my lips against hers in a kiss that was full of the passion and love we had. She was growing wetter, I could see the trickle of moisture running down her thigh. I pressed myself against her, the pressure growing within me.

Breathing her scent inflamed my passion. My body quivered with need. As I waited for her hands to find me, I felt her weight shift and a devastating sense of loss filled me.

My chest rose as I saw her rise and begin removing first my belt and then the thud of my pants hitting the floor. The sight of her firm tanned body with the curls of hair around her nether regions set me on fire. Then she pushed me on the bed and straddled me, burying my stiff cock to the hilt inside her warm moist center.

My hand moved down to the mound between her legs and stroked her g-spot. She groaned and began riding me. Slowly gently at first, then deeper, feeding the flames of my desire. My hands grabbed her hips to quickly turn her over, so I could have more access to what I needed.

My hands kneaded her breasts, then I took one nipple in my mouth and sucked as her back arched off the bed. I made my way down her body with my tongue. My fingers gently massaged her clit until I could get there with my tongue. My focus on her pleasure.

"Oh, God, Shane," she cried out softly, drowning in pleasure as her orgasm rose.

My tongue was busy, playing, teasing her g-spot. I gently slipped two fingers inside her and as my tongue licked in soft, hot circles she was pushed over the edge and her back arched as the orgasm rolled over her.

I mounted her again and with hard and fast thrusts brought her back to the point of no return for both of us. Her warm center allowing nothing less than everything I had.

We were laying there in each other's arms, in that comfortable time that couples have after a good romp in the sack when we heard sounds coming from Atty's room. Glad to have been able to keep our promise to each other, we rose, dressed, kissed and slipped back into parenthood.

Later that day, the gallery was abuzz with the vibrant chaos of an upcoming exhibition. Emily, her face alight with passion and determination, was everywhere at once—directing, organizing, and fine-tuning every little detail. I found myself in the thick of it, assisting where I could, feeling an unexpected sense of belonging among the curated chaos. The art, each piece telling its own story, seemed to echo the new narrative of my life—one where support and partnership were key.

As I adjusted the lighting over a particularly striking piece, a blend of shadow and light that reminded me oddly of my own internal struggles, I felt Emily's presence beside me. "It looks perfect, Shane," she said, her hand briefly squeezing my arm, a gesture of gratitude and connection. In her eyes, I saw not just the gallery owner but my partner, my confidant, sharing her world with me as much as I was opening up mine to her.

The afternoon waned, the gallery slowly transforming under our collective efforts. There was a moment, amidst the hum of activity, that I found myself standing back, watching Emily as she interacted with artists and patrons alike. Her passion, her vision for this space—it was palpable, infectious even. And there, amidst the swirl of color and creativity, I felt an overwhelming sense of pride—not just in her, but in us, in what we were building together, beyond the canvas of our individual struggles.

The moment was broken by the arrival of the postman, delivering the day's mail directly into my hands. The stack was routine, save for one envelope—thick, official, and unmistakably from the VA. My heart sank even as my hands mechanically opened it. The words "Medical Retirement" stood out starkly among the legalese, a final verdict on a chapter of my life that had defined me, broken me, and ultimately reshaped me.

Mixed emotions flooded me—relief at the acknowledgment of my struggles, a bitter sense of loss for the identity I'd once worn like armor, and a daunting uncertainty about what lay ahead. It was a crossroads moment, the end and the beginning, the final note of a chapter before the page turned.

Emily, sensing the shift in my demeanor, was at my side in an instant. Her eyes scanned the document over my shoulder, and without a word, she wrapped her arms around me from behind, a silent bastion of support. "We'll navigate this together," she murmured into my back, her words a balm to the tumult inside me. "This doesn't define you, Shane. It's just a part of your journey, and I'm here, with you, for every step that comes next."

"Thank you," I whispered, the words inadequate to express the depth of my gratitude, my love. In that gallery, surrounded by expressions of art born from pain, beauty, and truth, I found a new resolve. My journey with the military might have ended, but my journey with Emily, with Atty, with myself—was just beginning.

A few months had spiraled past since the day I held those retirement papers, each day bringing with it its own challenges and triumphs. Today was different, special—a day earmarked for family, for stepping back in time while looking forward to our shared future.

The fishing spot was just as I remembered—tucked away, a hidden gem veiled by weeping willows, their branches swaying gently in the breeze like the slow, comforting waves of a lullaby. My Granddad had brought me here, to this very spot, teaching me the patience of the wait, the thrill of the catch, and the peace of the rippling water.

Now, as I laid out our picnic blanket, the weight of my own fatherhood settled around me with a comforting, familiar weight. Atty, now more toddler than baby, was a bundle of energy and curiosity, his small hands pointing at everything, his baby babble a constant stream of wonder.

"Look, Atty!" Emily's voice, bright with shared excitement, directed our son's gaze to the ducks gliding gracefully over the water's surface. I watched them, mother and son, a mirrored image of curiosity and pure joy, and felt an overwhelming sense of gratitude. Here, in this cherished place from my past, I was crafting new memories with my own family.

Handing Atty a piece of bread, I guided his tiny hand to throw it to the waiting ducks, his laughter pealing through the air as they quacked and splashed, vying for the treat. It was a simple moment, yet profound in its normalcy—a stark contrast to the turbulent seas of PTSD that I had navigated. But here, in this role, this new identity as a father, I found a semblance of peace, a sense of purpose that transcended the uniform I'd once worn.

Our picnic spread was modest, sandwiches and lemonade, but it was the company that transformed it into a feast. Atty, between explorative jaunts around our little campsite, would come barreling back into my arms, his small frame fitting perfectly against mine. Emily's eyes met mine over his tousled head, her smile a silent message of love and shared contentment.

After the meal, while Atty napped in the shade, cocooned in the stroller, Emily and I sat side by side, the quiet between us comfortable, filled with unspoken words and shared dreams. My hand found hers, fingers intertwining naturally, as I reflected on the journey that had led us here—to this moment, this tranquility.

"It's beautiful here," Emily whispered, her head resting lightly on my shoulder. "I see why your Granddad loved it."

I nodded, the memories sweet and poignant. "It's more than just a place to me," I admitted. "It's a reminder of simpler times, of lessons learned. I wanted to share that with Atty, with you."

She squeezed my hand, her support unwavering, a steady presence in the ebb and flow of my recovery. Her understanding, her willingness to walk this path with me, bolstered my resolve to be more than my diagnosis, more than the shadows of my past.

Atty's waking words broke the reverie, a reminder of the beautiful, demanding realities of parenthood. Emily and I moved as one, a seamless team tending to our son, packing up our memories along with the picnic gear.

As we walked back to the car, Atty's small hand in mine, I felt a surge of hope for the future, a future where I could redefine my strength, not through the lens of combat, but through the everyday victories of fatherhood, partnership, and personal growth. This outing was more than a family picnic; it was a testament to the life we were building, to the legacy I hoped to leave for Atty—a legacy of resilience, love, and the enduring power of family. ***

The idea struck me on a crisp Thursday afternoon, right after a particularly intense therapy session at the VA. I was sitting in my car, hands gripping the steering wheel, mind racing with thoughts and emotions I'd unearthed in that small, sterile room. That's when I saw him—another veteran, someone I'd nodded to in passing but never really spoken to, sitting on the curb, head in hands. The universal sign of a man carrying more than his shoulders could bear.

It was like looking in a mirror, seeing the reflection of my own struggles in his posture, the weight of unseen burdens. It sparked something within me, an ember of purpose in the darkness of my own recovery. I approached him, hesitantly at first, but then with more confidence as I recognized the silent plea for understanding in his eyes. We talked, shared stories, and by the end, a seed was planted—a support group, not just for us, but for anyone who felt adrift in the storm of their own mind.

Emily was the first person I shared the idea with. Her reaction was immediate and unwavering support. "Shane, that's wonderful," she said, her eyes alight with the kind of fierce pride that made me feel like I could take on the world. "Let's do this. Together."

The planning phase was both daunting and exhilarating. I reached out to the contacts I had at the VA, laid out my vision, and found an unexpected wellspring of support. They offered resources, a space, and guidance on how to structure the group. Emily, ever the organizer, helped me design flyers and reach out to the community, her enthusiasm a beacon that drove away the shadows of my doubt.

We decided the group would not just focus on talking but also on healing through action—community projects, art, physical wellness—channels to redirect the turmoil within into something constructive, something healing. Emily suggested incorporating art therapy sessions, leveraging the network she'd built through her gallery. It was a perfect fusion of our worlds, committing to the strength of our partnership.

As the launch day approached, anxiety and anticipation churned within me. This was new territory, stepping into a role I'd never envisioned for myself—a leader, a facilitator, a beacon for others navigating the treacherous waters of PTSD. But Emily stood by me, a constant source of encouragement and wisdom, reminding me that this wasn't just about leading; it was about sharing, healing together.

The first meeting was a mix of nerves and raw emotion, veterans from all walks of life gathering in a circle, eyes flickering with the shared understanding of those who've walked through fire. As I began to speak, my voice steadied by the presence of Emily at my side, I realized this was more than just a support group; it was a lifeline, a beacon of hope not just for others, but for myself.

Together, we painted a canvas, a soldier's canvas of experiences and support, a network of understanding that stretched beyond that room, into the heart of our community. And as Emily and I worked hand in hand, bridging the gap between trauma and recovery, I found a new sense of purpose, a new path on the journey of healing—not just as a survivor of PTSD, but as a guide, a mentor, and a friend.

This chapter, this venture, it wasn't just about confronting the ghosts of our pasts; it was about building a future where those ghosts no longer had power over us. With each meeting, each shared story, each shared silence, we chipped away at the walls we'd built around our pain, finding solace in the shared understanding and common ground.

Emily's pride in my efforts was a mirror that reflected a version of myself I was only just beginning to recognize and accept—a man defined not by his war scars but by his resilience, his desire to help others, and his capacity to love and be loved, deeply, unconditionally.

In this new role, I found not just healing, but a renewed sense of identity, grounded not in the battlefield's chaos but in the quiet strength of community, support, and shared humanity. And in this journey, Emily and I, together, discovered that the truest form of healing comes from not just facing our darkness but from lighting the way for others, turning our scars into stars in the night sky of recovery.

***

The days melted into each other. Emily's laughter filled the rooms, blending with Atty's gleeful babble, creating a landscape of happiness I once thought I'd never experience.

As I watched them one afternoon, a serene picture of mother and son, a thought crystallized in my mind, clear and urgent. The realization dawned like the first light of day, dispersing the last shadows of doubt. I wanted this — this warmth, this love, this family — for all the days of my life. I wanted to make it permanent, undeniable.

The idea of proposing to Emily wasn't new; it had been a lingering thought, a whisper in the back of my mind ever since we had reconciled and begun this new chapter. But it had always been just out of reach, a 'someday' thought. Yet, as I watched the easy love between mother and child, saw the way her eyes lit up with joy and unconditional love, I knew that someday had transformed into now.

I imagined the future, a canvas painted with the colors of laughter, shared looks, and silent understanding, a future where Atty grew and thrived in the warmth of our joined hands. The thought of continuing this journey without the bond of marriage, without the solid affirmation of our commitment, seemed suddenly incomplete.

But how to propose? It had to be perfect, worthy of the woman who had stood by me through the darkest times, who had painted the light in a life I thought had dimmed forever. It needed to reflect not just our love, but our history, the pain we had overcome, and the future we were building.

I found myself drawn to the memory of my granddad, a man of few words but deep affections, who had once told me, "When you know, you know. And when you do, don't wait. Life's too fleeting for hesitation." He had lived a life filled with love and simplicity, valuing the moments rather than the grand gestures. And in that memory, I found my answer.

It wouldn't be a grand affair but a moment rich in personal significance, imbued with the history and love that had seen us through the storms. A proposal that spoke of enduring love, of resilience, and of a shared future filled with infinite possibilities.

As I mulled over the details, planning the perfect moment to ask Emily to be my wife, a sense of peace settled over me. The uncertainties and fears that had once clouded my future were now replaced by a sense of purpose and clarity. I was ready to take this step, to ask Emily to join me in a forever that was made stronger by our past, brighter because of our present, and boundless in its future possibilities.

For days, the ring burned a hole in my pocket, a constant reminder of the question I had yet to ask. It wasn't just any ring, but one that had belonged to my gramma, a woman of quiet strength and enduring love. Passing it to Emily felt like more than a tradition; it was a promise, a continuity of love and resilience through generations.

I had played out the moment in my mind a hundred times, each scenario different from the last. But when it came down to it, none of the grand gestures felt right. Our love, though tested by storms, had flourished in the quiet moments, the shared glances, the soft whispers in the dark, and the strength we drew from each other.

I wanted the proposal to reflect this, our unique journey from broken paths to a shared, hopeful road. It needed to be intimate, filled with personal significance. I decided on the old fishing spot by the Ocmulgee River, a place imbued with memories of my granddad and our early days, where tranquility met the steady flow of life.

The day was like any other, with the mundane bliss of family life—Atty's laughter filling our home, the warmth of Emily's smile as we shared our morning coffee. But beneath the normalcy, anticipation thrummed through my veins, every heartbeat a countdown to the moment that would redefine our future.

As afternoon turned to evening, I suggested a family walk, a chance to revel in the golden hour by the river. Emily agreed, her eyes lighting up with the simple joy of the moment. We packed a small bag—snacks for Atty, a blanket for us—and set off, our steps in sync.

The river welcomed us with its familiar song, a cadence that seemed to recognize our presence, a witness to the chapters of our lives. We found our spot, the memories rushing back like the gentle susurrus of waves against the shore. I spread the blanket, helping Emily to sit before settling Atty between us, his curious eyes taking in the serenity of nature.

As the sun dipped lower, casting a golden glow over the water, I took a deep breath, the ring heavy in my pocket. I took Atty in my arms, whispering a promise of love and protection, then gently handed him to Emily, our eyes locking in a silent conversation.

I shifted closer, my heart hammering against my ribs, the ring now a tangible symbol of my commitment, of the future I yearned to build with her. "Emily," I began, my voice steady despite the whirlwind of emotions, "from the moment I met you, you've been my anchor, my peace in the midst of chaos."

I reached for her hand, the connection sparking the familiar warmth that had been my salvation. "You've stood by me through the darkest of times, believed in me when I couldn't believe in myself. You gave me a reason to fight, to heal, and to love again."

The words flowed, a river of truths and promises, as I pulled the ring from my pocket, the heirloom glinting in the fading sunlight. "I want to spend the rest of my life with you, Emily. To grow old with you, to raise our beautiful son together, and to face whatever life throws at us, as partners, as best friends, as family."

I knelt before her, the symbol of our past and future held out between us. "Will you marry me?"

The world around us seemed to pause, the gentle lapping of the river the sole witness to this pivotal moment. I held my breath, watching Emily's face, searching for a sign, a hint of what would come. Her eyes, wide with surprise, met mine, a storm of emotions swirling in their depths.

Then, slowly, the corners of her mouth began to lift, a smile breaking through the shock, transforming her expression into one of pure joy. "Yes, Shane," she whispered, her voice barely rising above the sound of the river, yet clear and certain. "Yes, I'll marry you." Relief and happiness crashed over me like a wave, and I stood, pulling her into my arms, the ring now a symbol of our joined futures.

In the midst of our embrace, I felt a small tug at my hand. We broke apart to see Atty, his young face lit up with a mix of curiosity and excitement. "Does this mean, Daddy, you're going to be a real prince and Mommy a princess?" His innocence in the question, his belief in fairy tales, added a layer of sweetness to the moment.

Laughing, I knelt down, bringing him into our hug. "It means, buddy, that we're going to be a family, a team, forever." Emily's hand found mine, squeezing gently, as we all shared a look, a silent promise of the new, united path ahead. Atty, understanding in his own way, beamed, nodding as if he had decided this was the best decision we could have made.

As we lay together in the quiet of the night, Atty sleeping soundly in the next room, I found myself tracing the contours of Emily's face, highlighted by the moonlight filtering through our bedroom window. Her expression, always so vivid and warm during the day, now rested in serene sleep, a calm reflection of our shared life. In this moment, surrounded by the gentle rhythm of her breathing and the silent presence of our son, I recognized the significant strides we had taken.

The path hadn't been straightforward. There were times filled with doubt and shadows, instances when the remnants of my past seemed impenetrable. Yet, looking at Emily now, feeling the subtle presence of Atty nearby, I realized that every challenge, every moment of struggle, was worth it for the clarity and peace I felt now.

My mind wandered to the acceptance of my past, a complex journey marked by trials and triumphs, losses, and love. Each experience had shaped who I had become. The growth present in my life today spoke volumes, highlighting not just my own resilience but the steadfast support and love from Emily and Atty.

Thoughts of the future, our future, came to mind, filled with unexplored dreams and aspirations. I pictured the three of us, going through life's complexities hand in hand, a united front formed by love and shared experiences. This thought, simple yet profound, brought an involuntary smile to my face, warmth spreading through me at the prospect of the days ahead.

I whispered into the night, a silent pledge to Emily, committing to love, support, and cherish her, to be the partner she deserved and the father Atty needed—a pledge I intended to honor each new day.

As morning light filled our kitchen the next day, amid the routine and beauty of our family life, I suggested setting a date for the wedding. Emily's response, a look filled with love and shared dreams, was all I needed. As we talked about plans for the gallery and the PTSD support group, our dreams and goals intermingled, each word strengthening our connection.

But it was in these everyday moments, surrounded by the laughter of our son and the comfort of our home, where our deepened bond truly shone. In Atty's giggles, Emily's smiles, and our shared looks, I found real peace and affirmation of our journey together.

Discussing our future, filled with laughter and shared dreams over breakfast, I was struck by a profound sense of contentment. This—our conversations, desires, and the life we were building—was what I had always sought: a life rich with love, meaning, and the bright promise of the days to come.

Brushstrokes of Forever

Emily

In these quiet moments before the day began, I found myself lost in thought, reflecting on the unexpected proposal that had swept me off my feet. Shane, with his unwavering spirit and gentle soul, chose the perfect moment beneath the sprawling oak beside the river, symbolizing growth and enduring love.

The moment Shane and I announced our engagement, the reaction from my family was like a burst of color in an otherwise quiet gallery. My mother, with her endless enthusiasm and a knack for organization, seemed to have been secretly planning this moment for years. Her passion was a live wire, sparking with ideas and dreams, each call with her turning into a vibrant brainstorming session. She sketched out visions of the day with an eye for detail that was nothing short of a seasoned artist at work.

My sisters, each unique in their way, became the unexpected muses of our wedding preparations, bringing their individual touches to the canvas of our special day.

Lily, the middle child, with her practical sense sharpened by motherhood to two rambunctious boys, approached the wedding details with the precision of a skilled craftsman. Her suggestions were grounded yet imaginative, infusing the romance of the occasion with a much-needed pragmatism. Conversations with her were like watching a landscape artist at work, carefully choosing colors that fit the scene while ensuring the painting remained a reflection of real life. Lily's focus on the nuances of floral arrangements and her insistence on child-friendly spaces were reflections of her nurturing heart, ensuring that the celebration was not just an embodiment of love but also to family and inclusivity.

Then there was Elaine, the eldest, whose laid-back nature belied a keen eye for elegance and style. Her contributions were like gentle strokes on a mural, subtly enhancing the picture without overwhelming it. Elaine's laid-back approach to life translated into her ideas for the wedding – she was all for the feel of luxurious fabrics against the skin and the gentle, soothing cadence of background music. Her suggestions didn't come as forceful brushstrokes but rather as the soft blending of hues on a palette, offering a calming balance to the exuberant energy Lilly brought to the planning process.

Their combined efforts turned the daunting task of wedding planning into an engaging collaborative art project, each sister adding her unique shade to the overall picture. This vibrant exchange of ideas, filled with laughter and warm reminiscences of our shared past, transformed the process into a celebration of not just my impending nuptials but of the bond we shared as sisters. Their involvement mixed hues of joy and nostalgia, creating a prelude to the wedding that was as rich and heartwarming as the event we were all eagerly anticipating.

But amidst all this, it was Atty's role that truly framed the entire event with meaning. Our little boy, the heart of our small family, was naturally to be the ring bearer. This wasn't just a nod to tradition; it felt right, acknowledging his central role in our lives. Seeing his excitement, the way his eyes lit up with a mix of joy and curiosity, grounded the event for me.

This wasn't just Shane's and my day – it was a family affair, a celebration of the life we had built and were continuing to build together. His inclusion was a poignant reminder of how far we'd come and the bright future we were stepping into. This day, this celebration, felt like painting a new and joyful scene on the canvas of our lives.

We unanimously agreed that the gallery, a mural of our shared history, would serve as the perfect backdrop for our wedding. It was more than just a venue; it was a gallery of our lives, a place that had seen the spectrum of our emotions, from despair to unbridled joy. Translating it into a celebration space felt deeply fitting, blending our narratives into one harmonious composition.

Jenna, my best friend and the creative force behind so many successful exhibitions at the gallery, became the conductor of our wedding's aesthetic symphony. With an artist's eye and a curator's precision, she took the reins, ensuring that our vision for the day materialized into something tangible and breathtaking. Her approach was methodical yet imaginative, turning the space into a living, breathing art piece that spoke volumes of our love story.

Under her guidance, strings of fairy lights began to crisscross the ceiling, transforming the gallery into a starlit realm that promised magic as dusk fell. Vibrant blooms, carefully selected for their color and meaning, were arranged in an effortless style that mimicked nature's own randomness yet evoked a painter's careful composition. Each flower, each light was like a brushstroke on a vast canvas, contributing to a larger picture that was our wedding venue.

But perhaps Jenna's most touching contribution was the idea to adorn the walls with snapshots of our journey. Candid moments captured in the warm, unforgiving honesty of sunlight; soft, stolen kisses framed in shadow; Atty's infectious laughter caught mid-echo – these images became our personal gallery exhibit. Jenna orchestrated this with a delicate touch, ensuring that each photograph was a window into the love and shared history that Shane and I were celebrating.

Her involvement made the whole process feel less like a traditional wedding setup and more like an intimate unveiling of a deeply personal art collection. Jenna, through her artistic lens and unwavering dedication, painted our love story in the medium she knew best, turning the gallery into a sanctuary of memories and future promises for that one special day.

The quest for the perfect wedding dress became a memorable journey, a shared adventure with my family and Jenna. We ventured from boutique to boutique, each fitting room a new stage for a comedy of errors and moments of unexpected beauty. My mother, with her timeless elegance, leaned towards the classic designs, suggesting gowns that mirrored her own style from years past. Lily, ever the pragmatist due to her bustling life with two active boys, advocated for comfort blended with style, insisting that I should be able to move freely, chase after Atty if needed.

Elaine, the artist among us, favored the unconventional, urging me to try on the most avant-garde pieces that defied traditional bridal norms. Her selections made for some amusing trials, as I found myself wrapped in fabrics and silhouettes that were more at home in a modern art exhibit than at an intimate wedding. And Jenna, with her impeccable taste, subtly steered me towards dresses that echoed the elegance and simplicity of the gallery space, ensuring that the dress would complement the wedding's unique backdrop.

Amidst a whirlwind of lace, silk, and sequins, the opinions flew like paint on a canvas, each family member adding their own color and texture to the experience. Laughter echoed off the dressing room walls, punctuated by my mother's delighted claps, Lily's practical assessments, Elaine's dreamy sighs, and Jenna's thoughtful nods.

But amidst the sea of gowns and the cacophony of voices, it was a moment of silence that marked the turning point. I stepped out in a dress that seemed to silence the room, a gown that felt like a second skin, one that whispered rather than shouted. It was elegant, yet understated; a perfect blend of tradition and individuality, mirroring the essence of our gallery wedding.

Before anyone else could voice their thoughts, a small, awe-struck gasp redirected our attention. Atty, who had been amusing himself with crayons and paper in the corner, stood up and stared, his eyes wide with wonder. "Mommy, you're beautiful," he said, his voice a soft, sincere whisper that cut through the noise and opinions.

In that moment, all other opinions faded into the background. The dress, which had captured Atty's innocent and heartfelt reaction, was the one. His simple, yet profound affirmation was the only nod I needed. The search was over. The dress wasn't just a dress anymore; it became a symbol of this new chapter, chosen by the purest heart among us. It was more than approval; it was a blessing from the little soul who had brought so much light into our lives.

As the day drew nearer, each decorative detail added to the gallery was like a stroke on a canvas, each adding depth and emotion to the scene. The wedding became a living painting, each element a symbol of our intertwined lives, reflecting a palette of love, resilience, and new beginnings.

Beyond the tangible decorations, it was the warmth and unity of our gathering that filled the venue with a unique energy. This wasn't just a wedding; it was a vibrant celebration of life's serendipitous paths and the enduring power of love.

Standing in front of the mirror, stepping into the dress that had captured Atty's heart, I took a moment to soak in the reflection of my journey. The path to this day had been a complex blend of shadows and light, but it had led me here, surrounded by love, on the brink of marrying the man who had anchored me through life's storms.

The gallery had transitioned from a mere space to a sanctuary encapsulating our love, setting the stage for the promises Shane and I were about to exchange. And as our loved ones filled the room with laughter and anticipation, I knew we were on the cusp of something beautiful.

Today, I was more than a bride; I was a mother, a partner, an artist, embarking on a shared future painted bright with promise. As Atty, our little ring bearer, looked up with eyes full of trust, I felt the profound beauty of our shared journey.

This day was a celebration of us, our family, the intertwining of our stories. It was about the myriad forms of love that had brought us to this moment. Today, we were not just marking a union; we were illustrating our love's story, ready to immerse ourselves in every shade, every texture, and every moment of the life we were painting together.

TIDES OF DESIRE A SOLDIER'S CANVAS 169

As I stood at the entrance, arm looped through my father's, I took a moment to breathe in the scene before me. The space that had once been a blank canvas for countless art exhibitions was now transformed into a living portrait of our love story, adorned with delicate flowers and shimmering lights, each detail a piece of the journey Shane and I had traversed together. The gentle hum of our families and friends hushed as all eyes fixed on me. My heart composed a silent symphony to the love and trials that had sculpted this moment. I glanced at Atty, standing beside Shane, his small frame straight with a sense of importance and pride. His beaming smile was a beacon of innocence and joy, grounding me in the profound simplicity of the moment. Advancing down the aisle, each step felt like a brushstroke on our future's canvas, a path leading toward the man who had reshaped my entire understanding of love and partnership. Shane stood waiting, his eyes reflecting the soft gallery lights, turning them into stars that outshone even the art that adorned the walls. His gaze held a mix of awe and certainty, a silent promise of the vows we were about to exchange. The ceremony was a blend of tradition and personal touches, a reflection of our unique journey. When the time came for our vows, the room held its breath. Shane's voice broke the silence, strong yet laden with emotion.

"Emily," he began, "in this gallery, we've created a canvas of memories, painted with the colors of joy, resilience, and unwavering support. Today, I vow to continue this masterpiece with you, to cherish each brushstroke of happiness and to navigate every shadow with the light of our love. I promise to be your sanctuary, to honor and respect you, to laugh with you, and to shoulder any burden you face. Together, we will create a life that surpasses any work of art, for you are my muse, my heart, and my home."

Tears glistened in my eyes as I took a deep, steadying breath, feeling every word of his vow resonate within me. "Shane," I responded, my voice a soft echo of his strength, "you have been the unexpected masterpiece of my life, turning moments of despair into landscapes of hope. Today, I vow to be your partner in every canvas life presents, to fill our days with love and understanding, and to stand by you through every storm and sunrise. I promise to build a future with you where love is our foundation, laughter our soundtrack, and trust our guiding light. Together, we will craft a life not just filled with moments, but with meaning."

As we exchanged rings, Atty stepped forward, his small hands cradling the symbols of our union. His task completed, he looked up at us with a smile that mirrored the joy and love that filled the room, encapsulating the pure essence of our shared happiness.

With a nod from the officiant, Shane and I turned to each other for the kiss that would seal our vows, a kiss that spoke of past sorrows turned to joy, of individual paths merged into one. As our lips met, the room erupted in applause, but the sound that rang clearest was Atty's delighted clapping, his happiness a perfect benediction to the vows we had just sealed.

In that moment, surrounded by the people we loved, in a space that had witnessed the growth of our love and our family, everything felt profoundly right. We had turned the page on past chapters, stepping into a future painted with the bright hues of hope, love, and unity. In this new beginning, we weren't just husband and wife; we were a family, fortified by the trials we had overcome and the unconditional love that bound us together.

Canvas of Love and Healing

Shane

Emily and I arrive at the community hall, the crisp evening air brushing against our faces as we carry the supplies for tonight's PTSD support group. The hall, familiar yet always welcoming, holds a special place in our hearts. We step inside, the warmth enveloping us, a stark contrast to the chill outside. Together, we navigate to our reserved room, the space transformed into a sanctuary for expression and healing, a testament to our shared commitment and love.

As Emily and I start setting up for the art therapy session, there's a seamless flow to our movements, a rhythm honed by years of partnership. I pass her the paint bottles, our fingers brushing with familiarity, sparking that warm, comforting sensation that always seems to accompany her touch. She offers a grateful smile, one that reaches her eyes, and I can't help but return it with a warmth of my own, a silent acknowledgment of the journey we've shared.

I notice a stray lock of her hair falling over her face as she leans over to organize the brushes. Without a second thought, I reach out, gently tucking it behind her ear. Her skin is soft under my fingers, and she looks up, her eyes locking with mine in a moment filled with more than just gratitude—a moment brimming with the deeper connection we've built over time.

As we continue, there's an ease between us, an unspoken communication that needs no words. We share secret smiles as we recall past sessions, remembering inside jokes and shared experiences. Our teamwork is not just about efficiency; it's a dance of mutual respect and affection, a balance between two people who not only work well together but who have grown to understand and care deeply for each other.

As the veterans start arriving for the group session, the room slowly fills with the sound of greetings and subdued conversation. Each person brings their own aura, some with tentative steps, others with a more assured stride, but all united by a common colors of experience and resilience. They find their spots, some nodding in acknowledgment to Emily and me, others settling quietly, preparing for the night's session. The sense of community and shared understanding is palpable as we all come together, ready for the healing and expression that art therapy promises.

I stand at the doorway, pausing to absorb the comfort this room offers. The gentle buzz of conversation, the soft clinks of mugs touching, the rich aroma of coffee—it all brings a sense of calm. Here, my journey from disciplined military life to the unexplored realm of civilian existence, marked by invisible scars, finds meaning.

In this space, those hidden wounds are acknowledged and shared. I've found a new mission in these stories, these silent nods of mutual understanding. The triumphs here may be silent, but they're immense, evident in the smallest of gestures—a hesitant smile, the spark back in someone's eyes. These moments, they remind me why I began. Stepping forward, I feel an overwhelming bond with every person here, united in our collective healing. Speaking out, I welcome them, my voice a bridge between our shared pasts and our hopeful futures.

I turn to Jackson, noticing his jittery hands, and I'm transported back to my own days of restless nights and relentless alertness. "It's like you're always on edge, right?" I ask, my voice a mix of empathy and shared experience. I open up about my own struggles, the relentless sense of danger that followed me home, and how mindfulness, a practice I once scoffed at, became my anchor, pulling me back from the precipice of my own anxieties, offering a semblance of peace in a world I no longer recognized as my own. My story, raw and unfiltered, aims to show Jackson that he's not alone, that the path to tranquility, while uneven, is walkable—walked by those who once thought they'd lost their way.

Maria's voice quavers, a fragile thread in the stillness of the room. "They chase me, even in sleep," she whispers, a confession that pulls at the very fabric of my own memories. I lean closer, a gesture of unity, of shared battles fought in the silence of our minds. "I wrote them out, every detail," I share quietly, the memory of pen on paper, of nightmares trapped in ink, a method of trapping my fears that offered unexpected comfort. My suggestion is a tender offering, a beacon of light I extend towards her, hoping it might guide her through the stormy seas of her own night terrors.

Finally, Mark speaks of guilt, a ghost I know too well. Mark's admission breaks the silence, his words heavy with an all-too-familiar guilt. I see in his downturned eyes the same torment that once gripped me, a relentless echo of past decisions. "It can feel like you're drowning," I respond, voice tinged with the raw honesty of shared pain. I talk about the solace I found in journaling, how putting pen to paper allowed me to navigate the dense fog of remorse, offering him this strategy as a lifeline, a flicker of light to guide him through his own shadowed path.

In each exchange, I see fragments of my past self, finding healing in their healing, strength in our shared vulnerabilities. This room, these souls, they're my unspoken kin, bound by wounds and words, navigating a journey from darkness to light, together. As Emily starts the art therapy session, the room fills with an array of art supplies: paints of every color, brushes of various sizes, canvases blank and waiting. The veterans, initially hesitant, begin to engage, their movements reflecting their internal struggles and triumphs. I observe as they paint, noting the transformation from tension to release. Emily moves with ease among them, her words of encouragement a gentle balm, bringing smiles and nods of appreciation.

Throughout the session, Emily and I find ourselves locked in our own world of silent communication. I catch her eye from across the room, and without a word, she understands—she shifts her approach with a veteran, her intuition perfectly in sync with my silent suggestion. Our eyes meet again, and this time, a shared smile passes between us, a private memory of a past session where we faced a similar challenge and emerged stronger.

As a new veteran hesitantly picks up a paintbrush, our glances cross once more, filled with mutual pride and a shared understanding of the small victories we've come to cherish. These moments, these silent exchanges, they're our secret language, developed over countless hours spent side by side in this very room. They speak of a deep connection, a bond forged in the fires of shared purpose and mutual respect. Here, Maria's corner of the room is steeped in somber shades; her brush strokes are deliberate, painting a landscape that seems to mirror the turmoil inside her. The dark colors she chooses resonate with a pain that's palpable, pulling me into her world of shadows and whispers from the past. I watch her, seeing the silent strength it takes to confront her demons on canvas.

Meanwhile, Mark sits isolated, canvas untouched, the weight of indecision in his eyes. He holds a brush as if it's a foreign object, the blank canvas a reflection of his internal struggle. I approach gently, suggesting he start with a single line, anything. Emily joins, offering words of encouragement, reminding him there's no right or wrong in expression.

In these moments, the profound impact of art therapy is evident: Maria finding a voice in the darkness, Mark confronting the void of his canvas. Through these interactions, the healing process unfolds, guided by Emily's nurturing presence and the supportive space we've cultivated together.

From my perspective, the dynamic with Emily during these sessions is more than just collaboration—it's a synergy where our strengths complement each other, enhancing the group's healing process. Watching Emily with the veterans, her empathy and skill in guiding them through their art, reinforces the trust and safety within the group. My role transitions to support, both for Emily and the participants, ensuring an environment where everyone feels heard and valued. This partnership between us doesn't just strengthen the group's impact; it's the backbone of it, allowing for deeper connections and more profound healing among the veterans we serve.

As I watch Emily interact with the veterans, her compassion and dedication shining through in every word, every gesture, I find myself caught in a moment of quiet reflection. The way she listens, truly listens, her whole being focused on the person before her, it's a sight that fills me with an overwhelming sense of admiration. Her empathy seems boundless, her strength, a beacon for those lost in their own darkness.

I marvel at her resilience, her ability to remain a pillar of support while navigating her own challenges. It's in these moments, watching her, that I realize the depth of my feelings for her. She's not just a co-facilitator; she's the heart of this group, and increasingly, the center of my world, which includes our son, Atty.

My mind drifts to the journey we've shared, the obstacles we've overcome together, and how, with each challenge, my respect and affection for her have only deepened. I watch her now, her laughter like music, her seriousness imbued with warmth, and I'm struck by the realization that my life has become irrevocably intertwined with hers. In her, I've found not just a partner in purpose but a companion of the soul. My admiration for her transcends the boundaries of our work; it's rooted in the essence of who she is, and who we are together.

In the stillness following the session's end, Emily and I find ourselves in a reflective discussion. "Did you notice Maria's shift?" I ask, pointing out the subtle introduction of light into her once dark canvases. She gestures towards a canvas, her expression a blend of pride and hope. "See the transition here, Shane?" Her enthusiasm is infectious, bridging our experiences and perspectives. I nod, truly seeing the evolution she highlights. We then turn our attention to Mark's progress, his initial reluctance giving way to a hesitant but significant engagement. "It's a step," Emily remarks, a smile touching her lips. In this private moment, we delve into the nuances of each veteran's journey, acknowledging the role of art therapy in their healing. It's a shared understanding between us, a reaffirmation of our commitment, and a recognition of the silent, incremental victories not always visible in the group setting but profoundly felt in these quiet reflections.

Our discussion, rich with insights and mutual understanding, weaves a deeper connection between us, built on shared dedication and the silent victories we witness in our veterans' journeys. It's in these moments that our mutual respect and admiration become palpably clear, reinforcing the foundation of our collaboration.

One day, during a particularly tense support group session, a heated argument erupts between two veterans, each struggling with their own deep-seated anger and pain. I step in, my heart racing but my voice steady, trying to de-escalate the situation with empathy and understanding, reminding them of the common ground they share. The room falls silent, the air thick with unresolved tension.

In the weeks that follow, I notice a change. The same veterans who clashed begin to open up, sharing their stories and listening to each other. The group's dynamic shifts, becoming more cohesive and supportive. In a particularly moving session, these veterans apologize to each other and to the group, their vulnerability paving the way for a deeper collective healing. I feel a surge of pride and triumph, not just in them, but in the resilience and solidarity of the entire group, a testament to the power of empathy, patience, and shared humanity in overcoming personal and collective battles.

One night, as the last of the veterans leave, the hall quiets down to just the soft sounds of Emily and me tidying up. The afterglow of a successful session lingers as we stack chairs and organize supplies. Our movements are in sync, a comfortable dance we've perfected over time.

I lean over to sweep up some scattered paintbrushes, and Emily joins me, her presence a comforting warmth at my side. "You know," I start, breaking the silence, "today really highlighted the impact of your art on everyone. It's... powerful."

She smiles, a soft, contented expression that lights up her eyes. "And your words, Shane, they bring so much peace to the group. We make a good team, don't we?" Her hand brushes against mine, a spark igniting between us.

I nod, my heart swelling with a mix of pride and love. "We do. And your new show at the gallery, it's going to be amazing. Everyone should see the world through your eyes."

The conversation drifts to her upcoming art show, but as we speak, the distance between us diminishes until we're standing close, wrapped up in our own little world. Our gazes lock, and without another word, we share a passionate kiss, a promise of more to come.

Breathless, Emily pulls back slightly, her eyes gleaming with a mixture of love and desire. "Remember, Atty's at his grandma's tonight," she whispers, a playful yet suggestive tone in her voice.

The reminder sends a thrill through me, the anticipation of the night ahead adding a spring to my steps. We quickly finish up, the tasks now seeming insignificant compared to the promise that awaits us. Hand in hand, we turn off the lights and lock up the hall, our hearts and steps light as we head home to the private world we've built together, where love, passion, and art intertwine.

A Soldier's Canvas

Emily

The gallery is alive today, vibrant paintings lining the white walls, each piece telling its own silent, vivid story. The sun filters through the high windows, casting a natural spotlight on a particularly captivating canvas, its colors dancing under the light. I can't help but feel a surge of pride; this space, this sanctuary of art, is my creation, a testament to years of dedication and passion.

As I weave through the clusters of patrons, offering insights into each artist's vision, I feel the weight of my dual roles—the art curator with a growing reputation and the mother with a heart full of love for her son, Atty. I spot him, a small figure among the adults, his young eyes wide with wonder as he studies a painting. I pause, watching him, and the bustling gallery fades into the background. "What do you see, Atty?" I ask, kneeling beside him to view the artwork through his eyes.

He turns to me, his expression thoughtful. "I see a story, Mom," he says, and in that moment, the world narrows down to just the two of us, his hand finding mine. I squeeze it gently, a silent acknowledgment of our shared moment, our little bubble amid the gallery's hum.

As the day progresses, I balance conversations with artists seeking guidance, with patrons interested in purchasing, all while keeping an eye on Atty, who now sketches in his little notebook. I'm a bridge between creators and admirers, nurturing this space that has become a reflection of who I am.

Later, as the gallery begins to quiet, I reflect on the journey here, the trials and triumphs, the support from Shane, and the inspiration from Atty. This world I've built, where art meets heart, it's more than a business—it's a piece of my soul, shared with every visitor who walks through the door. And as I lock up, turning the sign to 'Closed', I feel a deep, fulfilling peace, a testament to the life I've carved out amidst canvases and dreams.

On another day, it's a quiet morning in the gallery, the calm before the storm of visitors. Atty, a bright and curious four-year-old, is my little helper for the day. His tiny hands are eager to assist, moving small, non-fragile pieces around, his concentration so intense that his tongue pokes out slightly, a mirror image of my own deep-in-thought expression.

"Mommy, where should I put this?" Atty asks, holding up a small, colorful sculpture that he's somehow decided was his project for the day. I guide him, showing him how the light catches the vibrant colors, teaching him about the interplay of shadow and light. "Right here, sweetheart," I say, pointing to a spot bathed in the soft morning light. His face lights up with pride as he carefully places the sculpture down, stepping back to admire his work. I can't help but wrap him in a hug, whispering, "You have such a great eye, Atty, just like your mom."

Encouraging him, I pull out some paper and crayons, setting up a small artist's station in the corner. "Why don't you create something for the gallery?" I suggest. His eyes sparkle with excitement as he starts to draw, his imagination pouring onto the paper in a flurry of colors and shapes.

Watching him, I'm transported back to my own childhood, to the sunny afternoons spent with my mother in her studio. She'd set up a small easel next to hers, encouraging me to paint whatever my heart desired. "There's no wrong way to express yourself, Emily," she'd say, her voice gentle and encouraging, nurturing the seeds of creativity within me. Her belief in my talent gave me the wings I needed to explore, to grow, to become the artist and woman I am today.

As Atty holds up his drawing, a messy but beautiful blend of colors and childlike interpretations of our world, I feel a surge of emotion. "It's wonderful, Atty! Let's find the perfect spot for your masterpiece," I tell him, echoing my mother's nurturing words. We choose a place near the entrance, where everyone can see his work. The pride on his face is a reflection of my own, a shared moment of creative connection that bridges generations.

In these moments with Atty, I pass on the same love and encouragement my mother gave to me, fostering his young talent just as mine was nurtured. It's more than just art; it's a legacy of love, creativity, and support that flows unbroken through our family veins. ***

In the calm of the gallery, Shane and I stand together, our latest project spread out before us: an exhibition featuring the art created by the veterans from our support group. The idea, a fusion of our worlds, feels like a natural extension of our shared commitment to healing and expression.

"We could call it 'A Soldier's Canvas,'" Shane suggests, his voice reflective, "to encapsulate their individual journeys." I nod, moved by the precision of the title, capturing the essence of the veterans' experiences and their use of art as a medium for expression and healing.

As we plan, our strengths complement each other perfectly. Shane, with his deep understanding of the veterans' experiences, contributes insights that ensure the art is presented with respect and sensitivity. I bring my expertise in art curation, focusing on how to best showcase the pieces to honor the veterans' stories and artistic expressions.

In one corner of the gallery, we decide to set up a collaborative piece, a large canvas where each veteran contributed a part, a tapestry of their collective journey. "This could be the centerpiece," I muse, imagining the impact of such a powerful symbol of community and support.

Shane wraps an arm around my shoulders, his presence a steady comfort. "It's incredible, Em," he says, his pride in our work evident in his voice, "You're making a space where their voices can be heard, their stories seen."

We move through the gallery, discussing placement, lighting, and how to create an atmosphere of respect and reflection. This exhibition is more than a display of art; it's a bridge between worlds, a healing space where the invisible wounds of war meet the healing touch of creativity.

In the weeks leading up to the opening, our collaboration deepens, our nights filled with discussions, planning, and the shared satisfaction of a purposeful project. The line between personal and professional blurs, our partnership strengthening in the face of challenges and decisions.

On the night of the exhibition, as I watch the veterans mingling with gallery visitors, their faces alight with pride and newfound confidence, I lean into Shane, overwhelmed with emotion. "We did this together," I whisper, feeling his arm tighten around me.

"Yes, we did," he replies, and in his voice, I hear not just agreement but a promise of all the collaborations, challenges, and triumphs yet to come. Together, in this space where art and healing converge, we've created something beautiful, a testament to the power of partnership, love, and shared visions.

The gallery, still humming with the echoes of 'A Soldier's Canvas,' is now a quiet sanctuary, the art speaking volumes in the soft evening light. As I walk among the artworks my heart is full, carrying its own new, delicate secret.

Shane, unaware of the news I'm about to share, is locking up, his profile etched in the dimming light, a portrait of dedication and love. The moment feels ripe with anticipation, a prelude to our next chapter. I wait for him, feeling the weight and wonder of our future in my belly.

"Shane," I begin, my voice a soft tremor in the vastness of our shared dreams, "the gallery show was incredible tonight, wasn't it?" He turns, his smile wide, reflecting the success of the night, our shared efforts.

"It was," he agrees, stepping closer. "But what's wrong, Em? You seem... different." His perceptiveness, one of the countless reasons I love him, sends a wave of affection through me.

Taking a deep breath, I reach for his hands, holding them in mine. "Shane, I have something to tell you," I say, my heart racing, "something wonderful." I pause, searching for the perfect words, but nothing feels adequate for the magnitude of this moment.

His eyes, always so understanding, fill with a mix of concern and curiosity. "What is it, Em? You can tell me anything."

The world seems to pause, the afterglow of the exhibition fading into the background of our life's canvas. "We're going to have a baby," I finally whisper, the words a soft revelation, a shared promise.

For a moment, Shane is motionless, his breath caught in the same suspense that holds my heart. Then, his face breaks into a radiant smile, mirroring the joy and surprise that I feel. He pulls me into an embrace, a haven of warmth and love, his laughter a melody that speaks of our future joy.

"Really, Em? This is incredible!" he exclaims, his voice thick with emotion. Our eyes meet, and in them, I see a reflection of all our hopes and dreams, the fears and challenges we've overcome to reach this point, and the new journey we're about to embark on together.

The gallery around us, filled with stories of resilience and transformation, now hosts the beginning of our most personal masterpiece yet. "I love you, Shane," I say, my voice steady with the magnitude of our love and the new life it has created. "And I love our growing family."

In this quiet space, among the silent witnesses of art and healing, we stand together, united in our love and the future we're building. The exhibition may have been a culmination of one journey, but for us, it's the dawn of another—our greatest collaboration yet.

Later that evening, with the gallery closed and the last of the evening's excitement settling into a quiet contentment, Shane and I sit down with Atty. He's buzzing with the leftover energy of the day, his eyes bright and curious, unaware of the life-changing news he's about to receive.

"Sweetheart," I start, my voice laced with a nervous excitement, "we have something very special to tell you." Atty's gaze shifts between Shane and me, a sense of seriousness tempering his youthful exuberance.

Shane takes over, his tone warm and inclusive. "Buddy, you're going to be a big brother." He speaks the words with a gentle gravity, watching Atty's reaction closely.

Atty blinks, processes, then his face splits into a wide, uninhibited grin. "Really? I'm going to have a little brother or sister?" His excitement mirrors our own, a shared joy that binds us even closer as a family.

"Yes, you are," I affirm, pulling him into a hug, feeling Shane's arms encircle us both. "And you're going to be the best big brother ever."

We talk about the future, painting a picture of a home filled with even more love and laughter. "Our family is growing, just like the gallery and our support group," I tell Atty, intertwining our personal joy with our shared commitments. "We're all going to help each other, learn from each other, and love each other even more."

Shane adds, "And this means we'll all need to work together, support each other." He speaks of the gallery, envisioning a place where Atty can continue to explore his own budding artistic talents, where the veterans can continue their journey of healing, and where our new little one will grow up surrounded by creativity and compassion.

"We have big dreams," I say, squeezing Shane's hand, "for the gallery, for the support group, for us as a family. But we've built a solid foundation, and together, we can make those dreams come true."

Atty, caught up in the vision of the future, adds his own plans and dreams to the mix, his imagination unbounded. In his stories, I see the reflection of our own hopes and aspirations, a reminder of the beautiful, interconnected life we've built.

As we tuck him into bed, his head filled with visions of being a protective, loving big brother, Shane and I linger at the doorway, watching him drift off to sleep. We share a look, a silent acknowledgment of the new adventure we're embarking on, filled with challenges but also with limitless love and possibility.

In the quiet of the night, our hands find each other, a tangible reminder of the strength we draw from our union. Together, we step back into the living room, the plans for our future unwritten but bright before us, our family and our endeavors interwoven in a beautiful, ever-evolving of life.

Want to read more from Lilly Grace Nash?

Love's Final Exoneration is the first book in the Brooklyn & Bennett, Attorneys-at-Law series.

When a man is wrongfully convicted of a brutal murder, Brooklyn Weston and Bennett Warren find themselves drawn into a case that will test the limits of their newfound partnership.

As they dig deeper, they uncover a web of corruption that reaches the highest levels of Monticello's justice system. With powerful forces working against them and time running out, Brooklyn and Bennett must risk everything to expose the truth and save an innocent man from a fate worse than death.

But in a town where lies masquerade as justice, will their love for each other and their commitment to the truth be enough to overcome the shadows of corruption?

Join Brooklyn and Bennett in this gripping romantic legal thriller that explores the depths of injustice and the heights of redemption. The fight for truth has never been more personal.

Don't miss out!

Visit the website below and you can sign up to receive emails whenever Lilly Grace Nash publishes a new book. There's no charge and no obligation.

https://books2read.com/r/B-A-WUJHB-YCGDF

BOOKS 2 READ

Connecting independent readers to independent writers.

Also by Lilly Grace Nash

Courting Justice
Alliances & Betrayals
The Billionaire's Legal Affair
Objection to Love
Love's Final Exoneration

SEALs of Love Romance
Undercover Hearts
Fractured Hearts
Healing Hearts

Second Chance Romance
Damaged Ex-SEAL's Second Chance
Ex-SEAL's Second Chance

Tides of Love: Military

Tides of Desire A Soldier's Canvas

Standalone
Billionaire's Nanny Fake Marriage
Silent Hearts, Secret Desires
Boss Daddy's Nanny

Watch for more at https://jllampublishing.com/lilly-grace-nash.

About the Author

My name is Lilly Grace Nash. I was born and raised in a small town in rural Georgia. Growing up in this close-knit community, I developed a deep appreciation for the values and beauty of simple country life. But even more than that, I fell head over heels in love with the enchanting world of romance novels.

Read more at https://jllampublishing.com/lilly-grace-nash.